TROPHY
HOUSE

This Large Print Book carries the
Seal of Approval of N.A.V.H.

TROPHY
HOUSE

Anne Bernays

Thorndike Press • Waterville, Maine

Published in 2006 by arrangement with Simon & Schuster, Inc.

Thorndike Press® Large Print Core.

The tree indicium is a trademark of Thorndike Press.

The text of this Large Print edition is unabridged.
Other aspects of the book may vary from the original edition.

Set in 16 pt. Plantin.

Printed in the United States on permanent paper.

Library of Congress Cataloging-in-Publication Data

Bernays, Anne.
    Trophy house / by Anne Bernays.
        p. cm. — (Thorndike Press large print core)
    ISBN 0-7862-8236-3 (lg. print : hc : alk. paper)
    1. Married people — Fiction.   2. Middle-aged persons — Fiction.   3. Life change events — Fiction.   4. Large type books.   5. Psychological fiction.   6. Domestic fiction.
I. Title.   II. Thorndike Press large print core series.
PS3552.E728T76 2005b
813′.54—dc22   2005026554

To Justin, as ever

As the Founder/CEO of NAVH, the only national health agency solely devoted to those who, although not totally blind, have an eye disease which could lead to serious visual impairment, I am pleased to recognize Thorndike Press* as one of the leading publishers in the large print field.

Founded in 1954 in San Francisco to prepare large print textbooks for partially seeing children, NAVH became the pioneer and standard setting agency in the preparation of large type.

Today, those publishers who meet our standards carry the prestigious "Seal of Approval" indicating high quality large print. We are delighted that Thorndike Press is one of the publishers whose titles meet these standards. We are also pleased to recognize the significant contribution Thorndike Press is making in this important and growing field.

Lorraine H. Marchi, L.H.D.
Founder/CEO
NAVH

* Thorndike Press encompasses the following imprints: Thorndike, Wheeler, Walker and Large Print Press.

"On the beach there is a ceaseless activity, always something going on, in storm and in calm, winter and summer, night and day. Even the sedentary man here enjoys a breadth of view which is almost equivalent to motion."

Henry David Thoreau,
Cape Cod

"To the untrained observer size often appeals more than proportion and costliness than suitability."

Edith Wharton,
The Decoration of Houses

CHAPTER 1

On the Wednesday after Labor Day, when most of the summer people had, thank God, left the Lower Cape, my bosom friend, Raymie Parsons, called me around eight in the morning as she did several times a week before I got down to work. Raymie is a geyser of gossip and hard news, a Wife of Bath; she knows people in high and low places and most of them are crazy about her, although she has her share of enemies, no doubt the result of excessive candor on her part. I keep telling her she ought to write a column for the *Banner*, but she claims it would spoil the fun, interfere with gossip's ad hoc nature. One of the things she told me was about this great meal she had had at Caro's, a place I avoid because of the noise made by diners ingesting the Lower Cape's priciest food and shouting at each other as if everyone was deaf. I asked her what she'd had. A Portuguese stew with five kinds of shellfish, halibut, sausage, and rice on the side. Then she said her evening was almost spoiled by a man who slipped the headwaiter a bill and thereby got himself seated ahead of everyone else waiting for a table. "It was so out there, so in-your-face. Before you knew it, he had the best seats in the house, you know, the table way back in the corner they reserve for Norman Mailer and Norris. That kind of sleaze really pisses me off. I suppose I should be used to it by now."

They refuse to take reservations at Caro's — that's another reason I don't go there.

"What's he look like?" I asked her.

"Well, for one thing, he was wearing a suit jacket. Who wears a suit jacket in P'Town in September? And for another, he had one of those trophy wives with him. At least she acted more like a wife than a girl-friend — you know what I mean, like she was a little bored. She was wearing tight designer jeans that showed off her butt, a skimpy silky top, sort of lime green, and glued hair." I asked her what she meant by glued hair. She said, "I guess it was moussed, not glued, but it looked sticky."

"High heels?"

"Probably Manolo What's-His-Name," Raymie said. "Here's the thing. Where have all the artists gone? Where the playwrights and poets? Where's the pastel tourist? This town is being overrun by people whose only claim on real estate has to do with gelt."

I told her she was being naïve and asked, rhetorically, when the world had ever been different. "You told me what he was wearing, but not what he looked like."

"Eyebrows," she said. "They were so bushy they almost covered his eyes. Black eyes. Very white around the pupils, like a kid's. He had one of those aren't-I-groovy five o'clock shadows. Have you ever smooched with a man who hasn't shaved in two days? He had a mean mouth. Look, Dannie, I may be making all this up. I only got a quick look. But the eyebrows — he puts Miracle-Gro on them and waters them every day."

"But the stew was good."

"Better than good," she said.

The one thing neither of us went anywhere near was that one year ago to the day the Twin Towers had been destroyed in the blink of an eye, sending most of us into a paroxysm of rage and fear and dreams of revenge (sometimes followed by an unexpected sense of guilt: what had we done to make them hate us so much?). I would have mentioned it if I'd had the right words.

Raymie ran one of the very few bed-and-breakfasts in Provincetown. There are a lot of hotels and motels, but only three B&Bs. I've always thought them an awkward hybrid, but apparently enough people want to stay in them to make them profitable. Raymie's divorced; Parsons is her ex's name, but she prefers it to her own, which she claims is too hard to pronounce. I think she secretly hoped that one of her male guests would take the kind of shine to her that leads to the altar. Raymie was fifty-one or -two and looked much younger, thanks to hours working out and eating the right things. She's not deeply into feminism — at least on the surface. She's always been extremely self-sufficient and opinionated, but she hates most labels, especially when someone tries to stick one on her. The only one she's proud of is "environmentalist." Whenever anyone violates the National Seashore Trust or pollutes — even by throwing a candy wrapper into the water — she pounces. She's a bulldog about saving the planet, undoing global warming — there's just about nothing interesting that Raymie isn't either for or against.

Superficially, Raymie and I are as unlike as Manhattan and Truro. She's a lapsed Catholic from Queens, where she was born and where she lived before her divorce. My New England roots go way back; my mom is fifth-generation, a Yankee who married her second cousin, causing a ripple within the family, but it wasn't enough to stop her. My difficult but admirable father died last year. He was a World War Two vet who lost the power of speech for three months after some harrowing action in Germany, then recovered sufficiently to get a law degree at Yale and use it profitably for thirty years. He left my mom comfortably off, meaning she didn't have to sell either her house in Boston's Back Bay or her place in Boca. She's a good egg, really, never comes to visit uninvited, tries not to tell me how to raise my children, and has no major health problems — yet. Some people call me a hermit, but I don't like to think of myself that way, mainly because it sounds as if I hate people, which I don't. I just prefer being alone or in the company of my husband, Tom; my children, Beth and Mark; Raymie; and one or two others. I don't much like parties, especially when they're big and noisy. Some people think that if you don't like parties there's something wrong with you.

I often walk around with a twenty-year-old Nikon hanging from my neck. I shoot pictures mainly of things and animals rather than people, who seem to freeze or act silly when exposed to the serious end of a camera. My favorite subjects are pale reedy grasses, dunes whose vegetable cover changes from week to week, houses in the middle distance, where they seem most isolated and, even if they're nothing special in terms of architecture or building materials, assume a kind of stalwart personality. It's like when you take a picture of a man in a roomy overcoat standing quite far off, with his back to you, he looks more interesting than he probably really is.

My husband, Thomas Faber, is basically a gentle, distracted person who teaches anthropology at MIT, an institution famous for its hard sciences, its supertechno-everything. So subjects like the one Thomas teaches are more tolerated than sought after. But it also means that his best students are sort of like members of an offshoot religious sect. They cling together. They have keg parties to which Tom is always invited; they go hiking together in the White Mountains and play penny-ante poker at least twice a month (at which he loses a relative bundle because he doesn't know how to maintain a poker face). Tom often lets one of them crash on our living room couch. They're slightly more polite than our own children, but they eat everything in sight and Tom encourages them to raid our refrigerator, something that really ticks me off, since I never know when or how many. This freeloading business lurks between me and Tom, and whenever we're tired or stressed, we return to it like an unhealed wound. I accuse him of being thoughtless; he accuses me of being a tight-ass. There's nowhere to go with this. A couple of years ago Tom won the Teacher of the Year in the Humanities Award.

We have an arrangement: I stay on the Cape from late April to November, and he's come and go. He spends most of the summer in Truro, but he also travels a good deal — conferences, consulting, other professional commitments met, I must say, with lively pleasure. He's not the kind of nature person I am. He likes watching the water come in and go out and he's fairly into birds — knows the names and identifying features of most of the shore birds that live around here. But he gets antsy after nothing but water and birds for two weeks or so — and off he goes again. Beth says, "Dad isn't very good at doing nothing." But all and all it works

15

out okay and we have, over the years, trusted each other not to mess with other people. I only did once, after a harrowing trip to the dentist when I was awash in self-pity. If Tom has, he has wisely kept it under his hat.

I quizzed Raymie about the clueless man at the restaurant because I thought I knew who he was. Abstractly, he was the enemy. If I was right about who he actually was, he had built a monster house on the bay side less than half a mile down the beach from our place, a house that was to nearby buildings as an elephant is to an ant. There you are, nestling in an area where the car with the most old beach stickers is considered much higher on the food chain than a new one. Small is precious, and the closer you come to inhabiting a shack, the better we genuine Truroites like it. Most of the older houses are gray and weathered and patched. What passes for gardens used to be the wild-growing rugosa and bearberry ground cover, but over the last few years some people have started planting heather and other hardy plants and flowers — you can't blame them: The urge to garden grabs you sooner or later — the need for order and color. The Cape wants color.

Just as soon as I hung up from my

conversation with Raymie, the phone rang again. The phone seems to have assumed a major role in the play that is my domestic life and fate. I can't imagine how people managed before the telephone. Your husband went to sea and maybe fell overboard and you wouldn't know about it until a year later and all that time you were writing him letters and knitting him socks and thinking what you would say when you saw him come through the front door and the fire that sex with him would ignite as soon as he took off his peacoat.

This time it was Molly Jonas, a retired New York advertising executive who works in the Truro Town Hall and is almost as good a news source as Raymie. In a small town, rumor and bits of questionable news float about as ubiquitously as those little white bits of fluff in the spring, keeping the populace satisfied. Molly wanted me to know that someone was building a swimming pool next to his new monster house, already in a choice location, overlooking the bay. "Another one of those weirdos, thinking it's going to cut some ice with what passes for society out here," Molly said. I was saddened to hear the swimming pool news, this trend toward big and lavish, toward excess as unstoppable as tax cuts for the rich under the Republicans. Bush *fils* was the kind of disaster you didn't even want to think about because you can't do anything about it — like a terminal illness. I told Molly I was getting on overload and besides, I already knew about the swimming pool, which was untrue, but I wanted Molly to believe I had got there before she had.

"I have to get to work. It's late," I said. "I'll see you next week at the Stop & Shop meeting." This is one of our more heated concerns: the huge chain market had threatened to erect one of its stores just off Route 6 in Truro. Most of the populace is outraged by this threat, largely — ignoring the obvious convenience it would bring to weekly food shopping — because it would destroy the more or less bucolic nature of this sweet little hamlet. For these people it would be like putting a Wal-Mart in the middle of Yellowstone Park. I have to admit I was partly seduced by the convenience aspect, not having to drive thirteen miles to the A&P, but I joined the protest because my friends would hate me if I didn't.

I'm an illustrator of books for children, books published in New York, mostly by Viking, but some others too. Once, long ago, I thought I'd be a real artist, but I've come to terms with just how far my vision could take me — though my skills are nothing to sneeze at. I've won a couple of small awards for my work and have more than enough commissions to keep me occupied until my fingers get all gnarled up.

When Molly phoned, I was on my way over to the dining table. This is where I work, because the windows facing north throw the best light into the house, and even though it means that whenever we need the table to eat off of, it takes me at least ten minutes to clear it of paints and pencils and paper and related stuff. I was about to do a first pass at a sketch for a book about a dog and a little girl who get separated in the park — a tale of suspense that seemed to me as bland as Cream of Wheat when it should at least offer its readers a hefty dollop of salsa.

Molly's characterization of this area as attractive to oddballs was not so far off the mark. A lot of singular types gravitate toward Truro and Provincetown, two communities that are nothing alike and that sort of bleed into each other. The opposite of hibernators, these people tend to stay inside in the warm weather, despising and shunning the trickle of tourists who come here by day-trip boats, partly to gawk at the gays and lesbians and partly to buy saltwater taffy and plastic key rings and teeshirts, and to eat themselves sick on hot dogs, fried dough, and fried clams. It's hard to sound good-natured when talking about tourists, but they do so often seem like aliens — and I don't mean the kind from third-world countries; I mean the outer space kind. I'm sure if you got one or two alone in a room with you, you'd see what nice, open-minded, humorous people they can be. It's just that I never have.

The singular people who live here are hardly clinical. They just don't always do what's expected of ordinary folks. I think they find the Provincetown and/or Truro air and light conducive to leading somewhat dicey lives. There's Billy Lawton, for instance, a man in his sixties who hasn't left his room on the top floor of a house in the West End for twelve years. There's nothing wrong with his legs, he just doesn't walk downstairs. He pays young boys to bring him meals and take out his garbage. He has a VCR and watches old movies. Billy reads a lot. He's also keeping what he claims is the world's longest diary, which he pays other young people to come and listen to while he reads it aloud. I understand it's quite amusing. Then there's Martha Ulrich, who was convicted of murdering her live-in boyfriend because he poisoned her dog. She served a few years in jail and now operates a one-woman band, very badly, in front of Town Hall where the tourists gather to lick ice-cream cones. You don't want to get into a conversation with Martha. There's a group of teenage boys — doesn't every community have at least one? — who go around after dark, beating up and rolling gay men. The police can't seem to catch them, but everyone knows who they are and who their mothers and fathers are. Two Provincetown men recently were suspected of lighting fires in beach-side restaurants for purely personal reasons — that is, each of them had a competing restaurant and probably figured a little conflagration was an efficient way to get rid of the competition. No one has formally fingered either person because the police are so inept that they don't have a clue as to how to proceed when there are two equally provocative suspects. Does this sound crazy? Out here it's standard. My last example is the shop-lifter, Sylvia Marcus. She's disgustingly rich; some people think her money came from a Neiman Marcus connection, but that remains an unproved rumor. Sylvia lives with her boyfriend, a local building contractor, on the ocean side in Truro. She climbs into her Beamer every so often, drives the fifteen miles to P'Town, parks on Bradford Street near the center of town, and makes her way from tacky store to tacky store, helping herself to seashells and combs and ballpoint pens and cheap sunglasses. Like the arsonists, she remains as free as a sandpiper hopping over the sand at low tide. No one wants to lay a hand on her because she supports several arts organizations perennially on their uppers. Wellfleet holds weekly square dances for the entire family on its pier; Truro holds a yearly dance in the dump, the place where Tom and I once watched as a semifamous psychoanalyst up-ended a garbage can into the hopper, then looking down into its depths, made a terrible face, and sent the can in after its contents.

But Provincetown and Truro aren't Sodom and Gomorrah, however often off-Cape people insist they are. It's just that, somehow, pushed to the edge metaphorically, a lot of folks out this way also pushed to the edge geographically and put down what passes for roots on the easternmost point of land in the U.S. Still, eccentrics are in the minority, and most of us just like living here for an assortment of reasons that have nothing to do with breaking the law or pederasty. There are thousands of men and women, retired from a life of hard work. There are men in the building trades, making a shitload of money, and who will go on doing so just as long as our town fathers and mothers refuse to put a cap on the number and size of the structures appearing here with the regularity of six-foot waves in a nor'easter.

I stopped working around noon and took our timid eight-year-old yellow Lab, Marshall, down to the beach for a walk. The sky was as blue as a Delft plate and almost cloudless except for a few wisps near the horizon. More and more people, I realized, were staying on past Labor Day, enough to make me uneasy. Figures, made tiny by distance, walked near the edge of Cape Cod Bay; a couple were sitting on the sand, wearing fleece of many colors. A man with bushy eyebrows appeared from over a dune. At his heels was a black standard poodle, clipped to look like a turn-of-the-century chorus girl. The dog calmly pooped onto the sand and failed to kick back over what he'd left there. The man was wearing one of those Irish tweed hats

23

of the sort favored by Senator Moynihan
and what looked like a brand new
Windbreaker. He paid no attention to the
dog, turned halfway around, so that he was
facing the water, unzipped his fly, and peed
near where the dog had shat. Marshall
started to growl and approach them cau-
tiously; courage is not his principal trait.
The poodle barked and showed his fangs. I
wanted to say something really nasty about
using the beach as a public toilet, but I
realized that if you pee in front of a woman
you don't know, you're probably not the
sort of person who's going to take too
kindly to the reprimand of a middle-aged
woman with no weapon other than her
tongue and a wimpy dog. The man was far
enough away so that his features were
somewhat blurred. But he saw me and
touched the brim of his hat in greeting as if
nothing at all had happened, and I was
abruptly overwhelmed by the rudeness and
selfishness of this man with his shitting
dog and his peeing and, above all, his
proprietary attitude: This is my beach. I
can do whatever I fucking feel like on it. If
I hadn't been through menopause, I would
have chalked up my sudden crankiness to
PMS. But I couldn't do that. Neither
could I explain it by blaming the huge

house looming nearby that seemed to breathe like a monster with its feet firmly secured to its cement foundation by iron chains. I couldn't insist that it and the others like it had changed me from a nice, affable, quiet person into a curmudgeon. Spiritually, I was feeling off my feed and the man and dog didn't help. Neither did the fact that it was a year since the catastrophe in New York and my unconscious supplied the memory so fiercely it felt as if it had just happened that morning. The air around me seemed to weigh more than usual and the sky began to cloud up. Everything conspired. And, even as I was aware of my superattentiveness and what for lack of anything better I'll call sane paranoia, I knew I was going to have to snap out of it or it was going to hurt me.

As soon as I stepped over the threshold, the phone began to ring; it always knows. This time it was our daughter, Beth, calling from New York, where she's the "Accessories and Makeup Editor" of *Scrappy*, a magazine for teens. She was making gulping sounds that nearly drowned her words. I finally figured out what she was crying about: she and her boyfriend Andrew had broken up and she was devastated. They had been living together in Tribeca for the last nine months or so and she was counting on their getting married. I asked what happened and she said that Andrew had told her he wasn't in love with her anymore.

"It wasn't even another woman," Beth said. "That makes it so much worse."

"You really think so?" I said. "I'm not so sure. This way you're spared the jealousy."

I heard Beth blowing her nose. "I have to tell you, Beth, I'm not nearly so unhappy about this as you are."

"What do you mean?" she said. "I thought you liked Andy."

"I didn't altogether trust him," I told her.

She said she hadn't realized that and this pleased me: I hadn't let on that I was frightened by his broad selfish stripe and his emotional distance, something Beth had apparently failed to recognize. We see what we want to see. Beth said she had saved up some vacation time and could she come up and stay with me? I love having her and her brother Mark visit, but I find that I use them as an excuse not to work. When there's no one here, I eat in bed, ignore dirt, and let newspapers pile up. So there are two sides to my children's visits. But how could I say no? My poor daughter needed her mom. I told her of course she could come up. Could she bring me some Stilton cheese and a dozen bagels?

Beth arrived the following day. She'd taken the plane to Hyannis, where I picked her up in the Saab. She looked as if she'd been dropped out of a window. She was wearing old jeans, a grimy NYU sweatshirt, running shoes, and a baseball cap over hair that didn't look all that clean either. If she was trying to hide her distress, she wasn't doing a very good job of it. She gave me a loose hug, dumped her duffel bag in the back seat, and got in the front seat beside me. I tried to get her to talk on the way home, but she wanted to listen to her CD player with plugs in her ears and I didn't feel urgent enough to press her, figuring she would talk when she was ready. There were a few snuffles and once, taking a quick look to the right, I saw her palms over her eyes. A mother suffers every pang with her child. It was not a pleasant ride for either of us. But when, almost an hour later, we drew up to our house, she seemed to cheer up a little. "Is Dad coming down on the weekend?" she said.

"I think so," I said. I wasn't sure myself.

Marshall sauntered out to greet Beth, waving his tail, and she bent over to fondle his neck. I took this as a good sign. There was love still inside her; Andy hadn't squeezed it all out.

We went inside and I started gathering up my art things to clear the table so we could eat off it. Beth said I didn't have to do that on her account.

She told me that she'd like to walk on the beach — by herself. "That's okay," I told her. I knew the virtue of a solitary walk: it does help you organize your feelings. Is it the sea? Is it the sense of the vastness of a horizon that seems to shift when the weather does? Is it the particular kind of sound when the tide is high, and its opposite, when the tide has receded half a mile, leaving the flats, as the beach at low tide is known, like a body with its clothes removed: all sorts of interesting things — shells, bits of crab, an assortment of seaweed, dead fish, an occasional smashed plastic cup — lying there, waiting to be covered up again? Whatever it is, I knew exactly what she wanted and it had to be sought alone.

By the time Beth came back from her walk, I had a vegetable soup almost done — I'm a cook who relies heavily on shortcuts and yogurt. She came bursting into the house. "What's that thing?" she said, pulling off her cap and coming over to stand right next to me — as if I'd done something nasty to her.

I asked her what thing she was talking about.

"That — whatever — that — I suppose — house!"

"Oh," I said. "You mean the new house."

"Yes," she said through her teeth. "Who did that? It looks like a halfway house for druggies or something. It's huge. It didn't look so big last July. My God, they moved fast."

"They actually had two crews working on it twenty-four seven," I told her. "That house has kept more tongues wagging than Jellies has." Jellies is the high-end convenience-cum-gourmet store that no year-round person would set foot in except in the direst emergency. They're too high and mighty to sell lottery tickets. The markup at Jellies probably hovers around one hundred percent — like four dollars and seventy-nine cents for a tube of Crest and five dollars for a slim box of spaghetti.

"I know I told you all about it in an e-mail."

"You did not, Mom, I would have remembered a thing like that. It's disgusting."

"You and I each have a different memory about this," I said.

It was obvious that in spite of her troubles of the heart, Beth was reacting to the house down the beach the same way I had, and the others who live here all or most of the year. To us it was far more than an eyesore. It was so out of scale and style with the older houses around it that it made only one statement, namely, "My owner has shitloads of money." It's a gesture of disdain toward its neighbors. It's the shirtless punk who crashes the formal ball, determined to be in-your-face and to curse while he's being escorted out. It works too — that's the bitter part. Once the house has gone up and the carpenters and plumbers and electricians have cleaned up the mess that's been a blight on the surrounding area for months, you can't kick it out like you can the young man with his pierced nose and nipple rings and no intention of dancing the waltz. It will be there until time covers it with a shroud of sand.

"They've been working on the place for over a year, but there's still a ways to go." I also told her I'd heard that the owner had built himself a house that was a sister to this one on Nantucket and then, because of it, was blackballed at the Yacht Club. So he sold it at a profit and came here where there are no clubs to be blackballed by. Molly Jonas says they're installing a burglar alarm. Beth asked what for. "Nobody I know even locks their doors."

"I guess to keep burglars out," I said. The whole community had had a not-so-mild case of the jitters since the murder, a year earlier, of Joanne Tinkham, a single mother with a small child, a crime so far unsolved and, from the looks of things, not likely to be, ever.

"You think you told me, Mom, but you didn't."

"Why are we going over this again?" I said, moving toward the pot of soup simmering on the stove. "There's no point in it." This conversation was now about whether or not I told her about the bad house and not about the bad house itself. This was not quite the way I wanted things to go, especially on Beth's first day with me.

"How about some soup?" I said, reaching for two bowls on a shelf above the microwave.

"What kind?" she said, reminding me that one of Beth's tricks is to manufacture tension between the two of us. I think it gives her a buzz.

"See if you can guess," I said. Then she

smiled and retreated. "Thanks, Mom," she said. "Andy doesn't do soup."

I had to sit on the words I wanted to say out loud, namely, "Oh, is that so?" or "I care?" But the poor child was pining for her erstwhile love. Who could blame her? Being dumped by a man is even worse than being fired from a job. I'm a feminist and I don't care what other feminists have to say about it — it leaves a wound.

As we ate — in more silence than sound — it occurred to me that the man who had peed on the beach the day before was probably the owner of the monster house. It all fit. The trophy dog and the hat and above all, his attitude. "You didn't happen to see a man when you were on the beach before? A man with hairy eyebrows and a dog. Not a lap dog, a big floozy poodle?"

Beth said she hadn't and wanted to know why I was asking. I told her I thought this man might be the owner of the house she'd seen.

"What's his name?" Beth said. "What do you know about him?"

"I think it's Brenner. He's from somewhere on Long Island. I hear he builds hotels, or maybe it's shopping malls. Everybody loves malls." Beth said that Andy didn't; he wouldn't let her shop at one.

Did she realize how bad this guy was for her — how he was taking small bites out of her? Probably not: I had the feeling that she hadn't entirely absorbed the idea that Andy was no longer part of her life. And for all I knew, maybe he wasn't, maybe he was just playing games with her and he'd be back. I kept my big mouth shut.

Beth wanted to know if there was a Mrs. Brenner. I told her that the word was, there used to be a wife. "They had three or four children together. Now there's a younger missus — much younger. Like a trophy wife. He's also got a trophy dog."

"Jeeze, don't you and your friends have anything better to do than gossip all day? When that weird woman was murdered last year, that was probably all you could talk about. Like September eleventh."

"I don't know what Nine-Eleven has to do with the Tinkham murder, but why do you think she was weird? How was she weird? I just thought she was pitiful."

Weird, Beth said, because she lived alone with a two-year-old off the main road and went to P'Town bars two or three times a week, where she picked up guys and sometimes brought them back to her house. "I call that weird."

"I call it tempting fate," I said. "And

you're right about the gossip. But it happened in our very own backyard. And no one knows who did it. For all we know, the killer may still be hanging out here."

She looked at me as if she thought I was going a little mental. "Well, you never know," I said.

"I don't know what's happening to this place — these hideous trophy houses and . . ."

I interrupted her. "Maybe it isn't quite so bad, pet. It's the way you're feeling about your own life that makes everything look so dark."

I had my work to do and Beth's problems were cutting into my psychic energy. That was how it should be, I told myself. This is your only and beloved daughter. But that same day I'd received an e-mail from David Lipsett, the book's editor, asking me when I thought I would have the drawings finished — in order to keep to their schedule, they had to go into production ASAP. Beth went down the hall to her old room. I could hear her taking stuff off the bed — I had started to use it as a storage place for some old jackets and sweaters and things like that — and opening and shutting drawers I had filled with some overflow clothes, mine and Tom's.

I spent about three hours doing dogs and little girls, suggesting a park with a zoo, animals and hard-to-read figures. I thought an impressionistic style would let the book's readers fill in whatever was wanted, from their own imaginations. I climbed into the box that was my work and shut the door behind me so no one could disturb me. I was alone with the silly characters of someone else's story and I felt like I was swimming in happiness.

Around five o'clock Beth said, "You have nothing to eat in the house — no wonder you look so skinny."

I suggested we drive out to the A&P in Provincetown and restock the refrigerator and cupboards. The shortcut I take goes close to the water in North Truro, a road not very much used, as off-Cape people don't seem to realize it's there. On this one short stretch there are two brazen new houses, twice as big as their neighbors. Beth said, "I can't look. What sort of people have this kind of money? Why would they want to live here? Why don't they go to the Hamptons if they want to show off?"

I told her she'd been away so long she didn't realize what was going on; this wasn't your ordinary secret Eden any longer; it was the Hamptons of New England. "Real estate prices have gone sky-high. We could easily get more than a million for our house."

Beth didn't respond to this, and I figured she must be chewing over the double-edged business of enjoying your plump cushion of money while recognizing, at the same time, how unfair it is to have so much when so many people are poor beyond anything we've ever experienced, poor enough not to eat more than one meal a day and not own one pair of shoes. Maybe it was better to be like the Brenners and not have a clue about the suffering in other parts of the world — or, better yet, not caring. Just being blithe about your appetites and your comforts. Dividing the world's wealth — one of the less successful solutions to unfairness.

The slim arc of Provincetown, resting on the water like a baby alligator, came into view as we rejoined 6A. The sun had spread a film of reddish-gold over the town, and houses along the beach were small enough at this distance to look charmed, like a landscape in an animated film trying not for ominous but for romance. "Wow," Beth said. "It never fails to get to you, does it?"

"I'd like to stop in at Raymie's for a minute after we finish our grocery shopping." Beth didn't say anything. I could tell she wasn't all that eager — probably thinking about how she'd have to explain about the missing Andrew. We had a good time at the A&P, fingering tomatoes, sniffing melons, spooning imitation crabmeat salad into plastic containers from the salad bar. Beth seemed surprised to see a Japanese sushi guy at the fish counter, rolling up rice and kelp. I told her this was simply another indication of the way things were headed. We bought some sushi for Beth. And a boneless lamb leg — for Tom, who likes lamb done outside on the grill.

In the parking lot, Beth said, "It's late, Mom, do we have to go to Raymie's?"

"I haven't seen Raymie in a couple of weeks and since we're here . . ." Here meant Provincetown. "I promise we won't stay long."

We stowed our bags of food in the trunk and then headed back toward Truro. Raymie's B&B actually straddles the boundary between P'Town and North Truro and was given the choice of addresses by the U.S. government. She chose P'Town because, she figured, for visitors looking for action no matter how tame,

P'Town would be a better draw than Truro, where there's nothing but wind, sand, sky and some old houses. Not even a downtown. People coming off Route 6 drive round and round, looking in vain for downtown Truro. One man was known to have driven around for a day and a half before he was willing to ask someone for directions to Truro, only to be told he was already there.

In 1989, Raymie bought a falling-apart late-nineteenth-century house that looked as if no one but mice and squirrels had lived in it for many years. She got a small-business loan and fixed it up with the help of shelter magazines specializing in before-and-after features — along with my kibitzing, as she called it — carefully following good ideas and discarding bad ones. What she ended up with was three bedrooms with queen-sized beds, one with a thin slice of water view for which people were willing to pay twice as much as for those that only looked out on trees and grass. She enlarged the kitchen so that if she's full up the guests can all have breakfast at approximately the same time. She chatted with them at breakfast, gave them tips on what to see and what to avoid, and did the cheerful hostess bit so well that no one could tell when she was blue or under the weather. "It's an act, Dannie," she told me. "But a lot of the time I really mean it. I really like my guests. I wouldn't be doing this if I didn't."

We drew up in her gravel driveway and parked alongside a Honda with chipped paint and a dented rear door. It had New Jersey plates. There was another car parked some ways off, a Lexus. As we got out, Beth reminded me that we were only going to stay a few minutes.

"God, am I glad you showed up!" Raymie led us into the kitchen, where she was obviously in the middle of preparing something for dinner. "Can you stay?" she said. "I've made much too much marinara." Beth threw me an urgent look and I told Raymie we had to get home for dinner; I thought maybe Tom would show up; I hoped he would.

Raymie asked Beth a few questions point-blank: What was she doing here? How was the boyfriend? Beth began to squirm and I said quietly, "Beth's taking a little vacation on her own. Can we leave it at that?" Beth sighed.

Raymie stirred her spaghetti sauce with a long-handled wooden spoon, turning her back to us but talking over her shoulder.

She complained briefly about not having the cash to fix the roof. Then she said, "I've got a real strange one staying here for two days. He makes me nervous. I haven't felt this way about a guest since that couple from Arizona . . ."

"The man who was wanted for mutilating sheep?"

"That's the one."

I wanted to know precisely what had put her off about her guest. "Well, for one thing, he didn't have any luggage, just a small backpack, not even a change of clothes, nothing. For another, he smoked nonstop, one cigarette from another. You know I don't allow smoking on the premises, but I'm sure he was doing it anyway. You can smell it." She heard him — through the door, of course — talking in an urgent voice on his cell phone late at night. "He didn't want my blueberry pancakes, just asked for coffee, black. He looked as if he hadn't slept more than five minutes all night."

"Something on his mind?" I said. Beth had perked up and was listening with interest. "How old is he?" she asked.

"I'd say mid-thirties. While he was out taking a walk — he said — I took a look inside his room — I had to replace some

40

towels anyway. He's got a detailed map of the Truro area and a pair of expensive binoculars. Maybe I've seen too many movies, but I'm sure this guy is up to no good."

"And what does this all add up to?" I said. I couldn't buy the idea that Raymie's bed-and-breakfast might be the launching pad for someone up to no good. I couldn't share her uneasiness even as I recognized that this person sounded fishy to me as well.

Before we left, I asked Raymie what she was going to do. "I think maybe I'll just give Pete a call, give him a heads-up. Not that anything's happened — yet." Peter Savage was the man in charge of solving crimes in Provincetown and catching perps. "He knows I have a lively imagination," Raymie said. "But he'll make a note of it. He's very obsessive about things like that, keeping track of phone calls and writing things down that might be useful sometime."

CHAPTER 2

During the drive back to our house Beth said
she thought Raymie was being theatrical.
"Why does she have to turn everything into
a melodrama?"

If Beth expected me to dump on
Raymie, she was going to be disappointed
because I wouldn't have even if I agreed
with her — which I didn't. "That's just
Raymie's style. She needs to give her
imagination free rein; that's one of the
reasons we get along so well. And besides,
this guy apparently was weird," I said.
"Give the woman a break. She works hard,
she owes big money to the bank. Can you
see yourself being chatty and cheerful with
strangers early in the morning every day of
your life? One of her guests broke an antique pitcher worth hundreds last summer.
So she just lied about it and told the
woman, who probably couldn't have cared
less, not to worry, that it was something
she'd bought for two bucks at the flea
market. I think I'd go nuts if I had to run a
B&B."

"Don't worry, Mom, I like Raymie," Beth said. I patted her left thigh and she smiled.

"Dad's here." Beth saw his Camry first.

Tom came out of the house. He'd had time to change into shorts and a polo shirt despite a furtive chill in the air. He looked pretty good to me. "Where have you two been?" he said, putting his arm across his daughter's shoulder and giving it a squeeze. "How's my girl?"

"Your girl is okay," Beth said. But I could see she was on the verge of tears.

"I hear the boyfriend took a hike." Tom sometimes has a way of being quite frontal. It didn't go over too well — as it often doesn't — but Beth managed not to lose her cool.

"What's for dinner?" Tom said. "I'm starving." He gave me a kiss on the mouth; he tasted sweet. Tom and I were apart almost as much as we were together. But he sometimes remembered to ask what I wanted; my friends tell me this is rare in a husband — and it's easy to believe, if you pay attention to all those jokes online, portraying men as stupid, lazy, self-absorbed, beer-swilling, tits-obsessed louts. I'm pretty sure Tom wasn't like that. We used to play games all the time, games we made up, like picking a spot up the beach, a house or a stairway up the dune, and guess how many steps it would take us to reach it. The one who got closest won. The prize varied. Sometimes it was an "immediate obedience," sometimes it was nothing more than a gesture of defeat, accompanied by a rueful smile.

"We hoped you'd be here so we got a butterflied lamb leg," I said. "Enough for three with some left over for the doggie."

We cooked the meat on the grill outside but ate indoors because of the chill, the dining table now cleared of the last trace of my art things, everything washed and tucked away in the hall closet. Beth seemed glad to see her father, who, having been prompted by me, did not ask her anything more about Andy. Tom hadn't checked out the progress of the house still being built down the beach but planned to the next morning, a Saturday. I told him about the meeting the following week to see if a group — "we're thirty-three concerned citizens" — could persuade those in charge to somehow short-circuit any plan to build more monster houses in Truro and to get them to sack building inspectors on the take, of which we had no evidence — the lot is too small, the dune is shifting beneath the house, the top story exceeds the legal height limit — except common sense. I hit a nerve with this; Tom is not quite but almost a libertarian and, although he deplores the impulse that makes a person want to build a house ten times larger, with three times as many rooms and bathrooms as they need, he doesn't like the idea of the government — any government — telling you that you can't build a house as big as Fenway Park if that's what you want — so long as it doesn't hurt anyone.

"But that's just it," Beth said. "It does hurt someone. It hurts a lot of people."

"How so?" Tom said.

"It hurts our sense of place and proportion," Beth said. "It hurts us just to look at them."

"You don't have to look. Try averting your eyes and look at the bay and the birds and the cute guys on the beach."

"What cute guys? If there are any in these parts, they don't hang out here. They're on the other side." She meant the ocean side, where waves sometimes reached a terrifying five or six feet. Whatever studs there are seem to enjoy parading up and down the beach in shiny black wet suits, their surfboards jammed up under the armpit.

It went on like this for a while, the conversation turning somewhat edgy but not enough to make one of us bolt from the table and slam a door.

But I went to bed convinced that the impulse to practice excess Tom alluded to did leave its mark on other people, strangers as well as neighbors. You can't do something shocking and expect it to leave no evidence, visible or unseen. It was like the murder of that poor Tinkham woman — still unsolved, and, from the looks of things, not likely to be. The clues were so cold they were frozen; traces of the killer were almost obliterated. It made us uneasy.

Next morning I worked hard and fast, managing to wrap up my assignment and get it priority-mailed from the post office before noon, after which Tom and I took a walk while Beth visited friends in Provincetown. It was a warm, clear day and the faux-Florentine tower in P'Town looked like a stone needle pricking the sky. Tom took my hand and we nudged hips. When he feels like it, he can be very sexy. "I'm over fifty," I said. "When you were a boy, did you ever think you'd be sleeping with a woman half a century old?"

"You're not old," he said.

"Maybe not ancient, but you haven't answered my question. Did you think . . ."

"Of course not," he said. "How about you?"

"I always liked older men," I said.

"My God," he said as we got near enough to the monster house to make out details invisible from a distance. "What are those gizmos under the eaves?" We walked across the dune and up the short wooden staircase slapped against the dune until we got close enough to make out details: the gizmos were small carved versions of shore birds, nestled up close to the overhang of the roof. "And get a load of that tower. Rapunzel is about to let her hair down from that window. What do they need a tower for? You'd think, given what happened last year, folks would draw back a little."

Towers, I told him, were this year's architectural necessity. "There are a few more between here and Wellfleet if you want to go look. Your house isn't complete without it has a tower. Now you understand why Beth and I are so upset. This place belongs in a theme park."

"We're trespassing," Tom said.

I shrugged off his misgivings.

We saw the house's owner before we

47

heard him and, apparently, he had seen us before we saw him — the man I'd seen on the beach, the one with the eyebrows like mustaches, had pulled open a slider and come out to see who was invading his space. The fancy poodle stood by his thigh. Marshall growled in a token sort of way and turned himself around to study some newly planted beach grass. The man said, "Can I help you?" in a voice that implied he'd prefer to shoot us.

Tom approached and stuck his arm straight out. There was no way the man could have avoided shaking the hand on the end of it. "Hi," Tom said. "I'm Tom Faber. This is my wife Danforth — Dannie. We live in that humble house over there." He pointed in the direction of our house, whose only visible element was the peak of the roof.

"Mitchell Brenner," the man said. "Met your wife on the beach the other day."

"Well," I said, "not quite met."

"Can I show you around?" Something had apparently made him change his mind about us. Probably pride of ownership had got the better of a naturally brutish personality.

I nudged Tom and said, at the same time, "We'd love to see it. Are you sure we're not disturbing you?"

Mitchell Brenner assured us we were not, although I sensed, from his briskness, that he had important business to conduct. He guided us through room after sterile room. In apologizing for the unfinished look of the place, he told us the outfit he'd ordered furniture from had managed to misdeliver, or not to deliver at all, the remainder of the furniture. He expected it by midweek. He cursed half under his breath, then looked at me to see if I'd heard. There was a five-person, L-shaped off-white leather couch in the living room, but nothing else. He made us poke our heads into five bedrooms, two of which had bedsteads with naked mattresses in them. The master bedroom was over twenty feet long and, like rooms in the rest of the house, featured a sort of pickled walnut stain on the floorboards. One wall was covered with mirrors. Lying in bed, the Brenners had that best of all views: the bay and Provincetown in the far distance. He guided us to the doors of four bathrooms, gleaming and barren, and an entertainment center with a gigantic wall-mounted plasma television set, speakers, DVD, VCR, and God knows what else. "We're going to install the dish next week," he said. My heart fluttered at this, but I managed not to let my dismay show. "And this is my rogues' gallery," he said, opening a door to a room off some room or other; there were so many I couldn't keep track of what he said each was used for. This was a smallish room with one clerestory window. The walls were almost hidden beneath framed eight-by-ten photographs of Brenner standing next to an assortment of celebrities and smiling as if he'd just had spectacular sex. Brenner and Dan Quayle, Jack Valenti, Britney Spears, an Arab sheik in full regalia; Henry Kissinger, Margaret Thatcher, Slobodan Milosevic, Michael Eisner (I had to be told who this person was), Princess Di. With Di he wasn't smiling but looked properly grave. Michael Jackson wearing a face mask. "All these folks stayed at one or the other of my hotels. Did I mention I own hotels? Seven of them. Three are in California and the Middle East, not the safest place in the world, but somehow they manage to keep running at capacity." So it wasn't malls, it was hotels. He pointed to a stack of leather-bound albums on top of a chest made to look rough-hewn but, as a reader of shelter magazines, I figured to cost in the two-thousand-dollar range. "I've got some more pictures if you'd like to take a look . . ." For a moment Brenner seemed appealingly needy. Then he snapped out of it. "Another time."

And on we went, into the kitchen, an area rather than a room, equipped with yards and yards of high-end counters topped by Corian. It had two double sinks, two ovens, a built-in microwave, a stainless-steel refrigerator, probably one of those subzero numbers and larger than a phone booth. Also a trash compacter. A small TV sat on the counter, ready to entertain its owners or the cook who worked for them. I thought he might apologize for having so much expensive equipment, but the opposite happened. "Ruthie's a whiz at this sort of thing," he said. "This kitchen is her baby." I understood Ruthie to be the wifey. I asked Brenner, who by this time had asked us to call him "Mitch," if his wife was here. "Not at the moment," he said.

We climbed a circular staircase to the tower. The view was all around us, a panorama of water and land, hills and a couple of boats bobbing prettily on nonthreatening waves.

"Isn't that something?" Mitch said, and there was no doubting his sincerity. He appeared to be wallowing in the beauty of

51

a view some people would cheat, steal and maybe even kill for.

He needed a shave, but he had been Eddie Bauered or L.L.Beaned in the casual mode; the giveaway for me was that everything looked as if he had put it on for the first time that morning — tan barn jacket, chinos, over-the-ankle boots with laces. He obviously hadn't learned that the true Truroite is recognizable by how long he or she can drive one car and wear clothes before they start to disintegrate. Or maybe he had learned and thought it was stupid to wear old things when you can buy perfectly good new ones.

I looked closely but covertly at Mitch, trying to guess his age. Judging from the lines around his mouth and eyes, and the loose skin on his neck, he was probably in his mid-to-late fifties, like Tom, but, unlike Tom, he was almost as trim as a boy and could be one of those men who work out obsessively to keep an incipient paunch in check. He had a mean mouth and close-set, unusually bright eyes, and those amazing eyebrows. There was something unpleasant about him — other than that he had built this offensive house — that made me certain I wouldn't want to work for him.

On our way back down the beach, with Marshall indulging in side expeditions along the dune looking for discarded picnic crusts to eat, Tom and I agreed that Mitch had done nothing that anyone could call obnoxious or even impolite. "He was proud of the place," Tom said. "He probably thinks we're envious because we only have one and a half bathrooms."

"And the countertops are cracking and stained," I said. "Well, I'm envious of his countertops."

I think Tom had difficulty believing this. "But it's not important," I said. "Rather our way than his."

"Do you think there's something inherent, maybe programmed into the human mind, that makes us need to rank ourselves higher than our neighbor, if not for wealth, then for moral muscle?" Tom said.

"You're the anthropologist," I said, "so you should have the answer to that one." Tom shrugged and changed the subject to our president, whom neither of us could seem to accept — although Gore would have been a less than lovely alternative. To me, Bush 2 was like a doctor you're consulting whom you suddenly suspect never graduated from medical school. Tom said he was a "stumblebum. He can't even talk.

And it's not a good time for working folk."
We didn't disagree about the Republican
Party, although he came at his opinion
from one place and I from another.

I was bored of the Bush-bashing I'd been
hearing recently and wanted to talk to Tom
about Beth. "Did I tell you that Beth told
me a little while back that she felt like a
married woman, even though she wasn't
even engaged."

"You did tell me," Tom said.

"Andy's too handsome for his own
good," I said. "He reminds me of Warren
Beatty as a youth."

"Beth always clams up when she's with
him," Tom said. "I don't think she wants
to hear this, but I'm glad they split," he
said. "Andrew's not good enough for her."

"But she's suffering, Tom, she's wrung
out. She used to be so cheerful . . ."

"Young love," he said, more or less
under his breath. Why couldn't he be a
little more empathetic? I knew for a fact
that he had had his own youthful heart
broken more than once before I came onto
the scene.

"She's almost thirty," I said. "That's
young compared to us. It's not so young in
the larger scheme of things."

"You're not going to start on that biological clock stuff are you?"

"As a matter of fact, I wasn't. She's got quite a few minutes left."

After lunch, Tom took a couple of academic journals out to the deck to read there, and when I went to join him a few minutes later, he was asleep with a magazine across his thighs and his head lolling against the cushion. Like Mitch, he hadn't bothered to shave and I noticed that some of the hairs sprouting on his cheeks were white. Old and tired. I still thought of Tom as a shy youth. Full of mental bounce and the seeds of immortality. I was obviously wrong. He still had a few years to go before sixty; at what point would he step over the line that divides middle age from old age? Would he end up gaga and/or in a wheelchair? Would he drool? Could I take care of him faithfully? Would I want to?

Meanwhile, Beth seemed to have cheered up a degree or two. "I'm going to call my brother and see if he'll come down for a day."

A few minutes later she reported, "Mark can't come. His band's got a gig in some Somerville bar tonight. When was the last time he was here?"

"Fourth of July weekend," I said. "The

same last time you were here."

"I told him about Andy," Beth said.

"What did he say?"

"He said, 'Hallelujah.' What's the matter with all of you? You hate my boyfriend!"

"Beth, dear child, we don't hate Andy. And anyway, hasn't he left? Didn't you yourself say it was all over?"

"I hate when you call me 'dear child,' " Beth said. Then, in a voice reedy with strain she told me that when Andy left he was in one of his moods. This was the first time she had admitted Andy was moody. But then she changed her tack and said that he would probably get over it and come back to her. They had so much in common. They liked the same movies and music; they liked, well almost, the same things to eat. His opinions about most things matched hers exactly. "Isn't that important, almost as important as great sex?"

I nodded, afraid that if I started to talk I'd get into something I'd rather not have her hear — such as my view of Andy as someone incapable of thinking about the other person, except insofar as the other person made him look good, someone wrapped up in himself like a little boy, a spoiled little boy. "Do you want to hear what I really think, or do you want me to

56

say what I think you want to hear?" At this Beth looked surprised. Maybe she was unaware that I was willing to be devious for her sake.

"I don't really know," she said. "Maybe I don't want to hear what you really think." I didn't want to scare her off, but my God, she was twenty-nine years old; when, if ever, was she going to learn how to use the tools life had given her — intelligence, humor, judgment, flexibility? Once, she had been the most resilient member of the Faber family. She was the one who told us the new jokes and brought her friends around to crash in sleeping bags on the floor. Now look at her: disabled by pain. Was it Andrew's fault? I had only words at my disposal while she had pain. Pain trumps words. It wasn't lost on me that she had come up here to embrace mother and father and substitute parental devotion for whatever it was that Andrew gave her.

It seemed I couldn't go to bed without one more call from Raymie. "That man I told you about, Lyle Halliday — if that's his real name — well, he split without paying his fucking bill," she said.

I asked her what she was going to do and she said she was going to report it. "It's not exactly grand larceny, but you wonder

— what kind of person does that? I knew he was bad news from the minute he got out of his car. There was something nasty about him."

"Poor Raymie," I said.

"I don't want you to feel sorry for me," she said. I told her I couldn't help it.

"How much does he owe you?"

"Two nights, that's two hundred bucks. Two big — and I mean big — breakfasts. He ate nearly half a pound of bacon each time — that's another five dollars. It's not the money . . ."

Whenever anyone says "It's not the money," it most emphatically is. But in any event, Raymie was out two hundred plus dollars and felt, as you do whenever someone steals from you, violated. "I could kick myself," she said. "He said he was going to spend another night and then, when he wasn't back by ten-thirty, I went up to his room to check it out. His room was empty, no sign of his ever having been there."

"I thought you said he hadn't brought anything with him," I said, feeling like a mean cop.

"Well, he bought a couple of things while he was here — a hideous polyester sweatshirt and a couple of girlie magazines . . ."

"You know everything, don't you?" I said this in a voice meant to tell her I thought she was sharp rather than nosy. She took it as such. "What an asshole," she said. "You know, in all the time I've had this place, no one has ever stiffed me before."

"You must be blessed," I said.

The next day, Sunday, I drove over to see Raymie, leaving Tom with his journals. By this time Raymie had lost some of her fury and was busy cleaning up after breakfast for two guests. "Blueberry pancakes," she said. "I had to buy frozen berries. They think 'cause it's the Cape that we have berries year-round."

I asked her if she'd spoken to Pete Savage, her friend on the police force. Not only spoken to him but had gone to the police headquarters where she signed a complaint that fingered Halliday — or whatever his name was. Savage told Raymie the amount of money she was out was too small to trigger an official investigation. Just petty larceny, no big deal. "He told me there are so many similar incidents every summer that they'd had to upgrade their computer's memory just to keep the database on shoplifters and people who stiffed their landlords up to date."

"We seem to attract weirdos," Beth said.

"One of my guests claims our zip code is bad luck, the number's — get this — Satanic. I told him I'd lived in 666 for a decade without anything dire happening, and I suggested that people who live their lives using superstition as a handbook were wasting a hell of a lot of energy. Well, I didn't exactly say it that way. I just told him I wasn't superstitious."

When I got back to our house, I told Tom what had happened.

Tom's response: "She needs a boyfriend. She should have had children."

This wasn't exactly what I expected, and its simplicity — and its implied sexism — ticked me off, but I resisted the urge to tell him so. But then, as I began to think about it, I realized that he was probably right; children certainly focus your mind — even when you'd rather be thinking about something else. It never ends.

Tom spent the rest of the day doing chores I didn't feel up to, activities that involved lifting, hammering, replacing, gathering of heavy objects. He's never liked this sort of work especially, so I was properly grateful. "Do you have to go back?" I said as we sat on the deck after dinner. I knew he had a class to teach the following day, but I asked him anyway.

"You know I do," he said. "And Mark's meeting me for dinner."

I said something about September being the best month on the Cape.

He knows how I feel about spending the fall here, when one layer of the community — the summer people — is shed like the skin of a snake, leaving us to what's raw and thereby lovely underneath. Is it "realer" or is that just my imagining? Fantasy or not, as soon as the summer people leave, I wake up happier, feeling more like a natural child — although that too is a fantasy.

"I'll be back next Friday," Tom said. I thought he was about to reach for my hand, but I was wrong.

Beth was still asleep when I got up at six the next morning with Tom, brewed a pot of coffee and scrambled some eggs for him. The eggs come from one of the few working farms left on the Outer Cape. I find it peculiar how we adhere to these old-fashioned emblems: eggs dropped directly into our palms, well water; shampoo made with distilled essence of something — as if they made any real difference in our lives, already so fraught with risk: cars hurtling down Route 6 (I knew personally four people killed on the spot in Route 6 accidents); maniacs with mini atom bombs inside suitcases; AIDS. "Fresh from the farm," I told Tom as I served them up with six-grain bread and homemade blueberry preserves (homemade by someone else). He ate quickly, mumbling something about not being quite prepared for his first class. The shadow of anxiety crossed his features. "You'll do fine," I said. "You always have."

After he left, I realized that my spirits — pretty bright that morning — were no different with him gone. I didn't mind his leaving. This frightened me. That some kind of worm had crawled into the apple was a reality I couldn't ignore. When a marriage goes sour, it doesn't do it all at once; it does it over days, weeks, months, maybe years, so gradually that you're not sure you're not imagining things. My cousin Caroline, a woman I rarely see precisely because of what she said to me, said to me that the reason Tom and I stayed married when everyone else seemed to be on their second or third spouse was that we were apart so much. "You're not lovebirds at all," Caroline told me. "You're ships that pass in the night." I hadn't asked for her opinion. I sent her a postcard: "Congratulations. You've just won our Tactless Remark of the Month Award. You have been automatically entered in our annual contest." The next time I saw her, she pretended not to see me.

When Beth came out of her room, bed-headed and sleepy-looking, like the little girl she was long ago, I wanted to hug her. "Has Dad left already?"

"It's after nine," I said. "He's already in the classroom."

"Don't you mind it when he leaves?" she asked me.

"Sure I do," I said. "But look, if I were back in Watertown, I wouldn't be seeing him during the day anyway. This way, I get to be here, and you know I like being alone to do my work and take my walks, to do my little things. And to think."

Beth, clever girl, looked at me as if I was hiding something from her — as I was. I told her I had to get to work on another assignment, this one from Little, Brown, not due for another three months, but I'm the sort of person who, if she doesn't work every weekday, falls into sloth and indolence.

Beth left for a beach walk; she was doing a lot of thinking herself and sorting things that I guessed were not easily sortable.

Sighing for her, I reread the book I was supposed to be illustrating for about the tenth time, trying to pull in ideas from wherever it is ideas reside. The story was about a ten-year-old boy named Chris who flies from Philadelphia to San Francisco by himself, changing planes in Chicago. Like so many books I do the pictures for, this one contains an upbeat message: you can do anything you put your mind to, even something so scary you can hardly breathe. What bothered me about the story was that nothing unexpected happened. Chris's mother deposits him on the plane with a pile of games and reading, the flight attendant puts him on the second plane, his grandmother meets him at the San Francisco airport. He eats three times, goes to the bathroom twice, talks to the nice man in the next seat, walks through O'Hare, browses in a gift shop where he buys a key ring for his mother. That's it. No missed connections, no turbulence, not a moment of suspense. If and when I have grandchildren, I'm not going to read them *Christopher Is Airborne*. It's Grimms' fairy tales or *Struwwelpeter* or nothing.

Beth came back just as I was finishing up my work. The beach had been almost hers, she reported. It was like having your own private seashore, except for this one man who made her feel weird. He kept staring at the monster house, then walking away, then walking back and staring some more. "When he saw me, he looked at me that funny way, like he was seeing and not seeing me at the same time. It was, like, I was there but invisible." I asked Beth what the man looked like. How old did she think? How was he dressed? Without having laid my eyes on Raymie's thief, I was pretty sure the man Beth had seen and Lyle Halliday were, as Sherlock Holmes might say in one of his moments, "one and the same."

Right away I got Raymie on the phone. Then I put Beth on with her. Beth talked excitedly to Raymie, then hung up. "It's him!" she said, caught up in the thrill of this pursuit. "She's going to get in touch with the P'Town police and then come over to Truro."

I suggested we go back down to the beach. When we got there, the man had vanished. "Bummer," Beth said. "I was looking forward to a little excitement."

She was not to be disappointed. As we drew closer to the house, we saw a man strapped into a narrow chair being lifted up the stairway that connected house and beach, by three men, one guiding the other two, the actual carriers. A woman I guessed was Ruthie, the wife, brought up the rear, waving her arms and yelling something I couldn't quite make out. "That's Mitchell Brenner," I said.

"You mean the guy who owns that horrible house?"

"That one. He looks like he was hit by a bus."

"Let's find out what happened," Beth said.

"I don't think so."

"Why not?"

"I can't tell you exactly. It just doesn't seem like the right thing to do. We hardly know him, and I haven't even met her. Come on, we'll go back to the house, where I'll bet you anything the phone will be ringing."

We walked back up the beach. Shaky from what we had just seen, I poured each of us a glass of wine. I couldn't throw off the feeling that things were out of control, that there were too many creases on the once-smooth sheet of my Truro life. The anniversary of the catastrophe in New York, Beth's pain, Raymie's theft, the accident down the beach. I felt as if time were quickening, as if the planet were turning on its axis too fast and the centrifugal force would spin us off its gravity. I held on to the counter and said, "What next?"

CHAPTER 3

Whenever I'm faced with something I can't understand, I open the door of her cage and release my imagination. She still flies with relative ease, though her wings are somewhat frayed. I think she enjoys the pain involved in drawing the most lurid picture to explain it: buckets of blood, jagged edges, buildings turned to rubble, flames, torn bodies, corpses strewn over the landscape. Because whatever money I make, I make by using my imagination, and because this picturing the ugliest possible scenario is a habit of long standing — triggered, I'm certain, by the scene in the movie of *Gone with the Wind* where men writhe on the ground, shrieking, outside an Atlanta hospital — I went with the worst possible scenario: someone had tried to kill Mitchell Brenner — and probably because they hated his house.

Sometime later Raymie drove over from P'Town, parked her car at Ryder Beach and walked up to the Brenner place, where she was told to leave *"now"* by two Truro cops as they symbolically contained the property in yellow plastic tape — "Crime Scene." But before she did that, she was on the phone with her pal, the Provincetown cop, who told her that someone had splashed blood — or pretty good red paint — all over the front of the Brenner house, buckets of it apparently. Then he'd taken a large brush and written JEW PIG on the front door. "Nice, huh?" Raymie said.

"Yes, but how did Brenner end up hurt?" I said.

"Apparently, he caught sight of Halliday just as he was taking off and ran after him. He slipped on the stairs and fell halfway down. They think he broke one or both legs pretty bad."

I was surprised to hear that Mitch Brenner was Jewish. "I'm not sure whether he is or isn't," Raymie said. "But that creep, Halliday, apparently isn't. Fucking anti-Semite! What's happening to this place? Things like this never used to happen."

I reminded her about the Tinkham murder, still unsolved. The idea that Halliday was loose in the neighborhood made me extremely nervous. Raymie said, "Can I have some of that?" pointing to the wine. I got her a glass. She sat down on the couch and slipped into a thoughtful mode. "And speaking of Jews," she said, "that yellow tape made me think of an eruv. That's a hugely long piece of string observant Jews use to sort of cordon off an area — sometimes an entire town — inside of which they are permitted to violate rules of the Jewish Sabbath. My cousin Ellen married an Orthodox Jew — and incidentally got read out of the family until she got pregnant. Then all was forgiven. Ellen told me about this eruv thing. It's basically a weasel, if you ask me. Either you obey the rules or you don't. You shouldn't try to get around them. I said as much to Ellen and she had the nerve to tell me I wouldn't understand. Don't you love it?" Raymie — who feels right at home in my house — got up and made us some iced tea. "I probably shouldn't be saying this, but this Brenner guy with his fat wallet and bad attitude was asking for it."

"You sound like one of those redneck judges who tell the rape victim she was wearing 'inappropriate' clothes . . ."

"Something like that," Raymie said.

"I think that's BS, if you don't mind me saying so," Beth said. "The girl doesn't ask for it."

"Never?"

I didn't enjoy hearing Raymie talk like this. A new Raymie. Where had she come from? And, more to the point, why? Or maybe she had been like this all along and I was too dense to see it.

For the second time since the end of August, Raymie had no paying guests. She tried to pretend it didn't matter, but I could tell she wasn't exactly thrilled about it. She needed the money.

The three of us sat around, suspended in inactivity and small talk while the afternoon wore itself out. I called Tom, who said he was sorry he wasn't here with me. "Please don't let it get to you, Dannie. If I tell you it's not really our business, I know what you'll answer so I won't say it. But try not to overreact." This struck me as a supremely silly instruction. How else could I be expected to act when something awful happens to a neighbor, no matter how unappetizing he happens to be?

We ignored the gorgeous sunset and then, I suppose inevitably, as anniversaries always stir up the unconscious, started talking about what had happened a year ago. "It's like there's this big gray shadow over us, the way it was in the City. Even here, where we're probably safe," Beth said. It had taken me two days to reach her by phone. By the time I finally got through to her, I was a basket case. She was horribly upset; from her office window she had seen the towers go down.

We ate a meal of leftover vegetables piled on angel hair spaghetti — pretty good, if you ask me. I sometimes think I should change my game and be a chef. We tried to talk about other things and kept returning to Mitch Brenner and his house, as if talking about it would hold it steady. At one point I said, "Most of the time, we don't get to see anything really awful. We know someone who knew someone who saw a crime being committed, but that's already one step away. People like us are cushioned. Somehow we manage not to stumble over the corpse on the beach. I know all these people are killed on Route 6, but I've never actually seen a car crash." Raymie said she'd seen one and that it was nothing you'd want to remember. "The driver's head was sheared off not twenty feet from where I'd stopped my car. You know that place where you're making a left-hand turn across the opposite lane, to get to Wellfleet Center? Well, this guy was in a convertible and he ran a red light and this other car was making the turn and they crashed head-on. I still see it sometimes when I can't sleep at night . . ." Beth, it turned out, had been near enough to get the visual gist of a knife fight between two teenagers in Tribeca. "They took one of the kids to the hospital," she said. "You know how they say 'It left me shaking'? Well, it left me shaking — and I didn't even know them." I thought of her living in a place where people settled disagreements with knives and it made me tremble for her.

"How come you never told me that before?" I said.

"I guess I forgot," she said. But I'm certain she meant she didn't want to have to deal with my anxiety, a faculty that occasionally gets out of hand.

Raymie's cell phone did an aria. She pulled it out of her purse, unfolded it and answered. She listened briefly, then said, "They took Brenner to Hyannis. Pete says it's both legs, but they think he's going to be okay."

I thought how convenient it was for Raymie to have a direct line to behind-the-scenes at police headquarters. "By the way, Pete's fairly certain it was Lyle Halliday," Raymie said. "All the pieces fit."

"It fits too well," I said. "It's too obvious."

"No such thing as too obvious," Raymie

said. "Haven't you read Sherlock Holmes?"

"I know," Beth said brightly. "He hated the trophy house. He couldn't stomach what it stood for. He was like an activist, an ecoterrorist and a Nazi. To say nothing of his being a whack job."

"Interesting combination," Raymie said.

"We don't know anything yet," I said, more upset by what had happened than I probably should have been. Violence had stopped in at Truro again for the second time in just over two years. Why should we be exempt? We pride ourselves on leaving our front doors unlocked and being able to stand in the moonlight without fear of being mugged. Excepting the Tinkham murder, nothing dire had occurred here in more than thirty years, not since a nut named Costa went on a killing spree and buried two of his female victims in the local cemetery. It's not exactly pride — it's more like complacency.

Finally, around ten o'clock, Raymie left and Beth and I went to bed. Whenever Tom wasn't here, I swung my legs over to where he should be lying, half-liking the emptiness. After a few rough years we had arrived at our accommodation together. It was a plan that fell short of perfection for both of us, but if we hadn't decided on a split life, the only other choices would have been for one of us to cave completely or else get a divorce.

When I woke up the next morning, I knew right away, from the brightness of the light inside our bedroom and the way it boldly crossed the floor and hit the glass over a watercolor of Provincetown Harbor, where human dwellings are the size of baby snails — but you can tell exactly what the artist saw and why he wanted you to see it this way — I knew it was one of those crystalline days that happen mostly in April and early fall. When I looked out over the bay, I thought I had only once before, exactly a year ago, seen a sky so coherently blue; the blueness seemed double-strength and there wasn't a wisp of cloud or haze to blot it. Beth noticed it too. "Just like last year," she said. "We don't have skies like this in New York very often. Sometimes I don't know why I like living there."

"You can't eat the sky," I said. "You can't hold a conversation with it. You can't make a living off it."

Beth wouldn't let me fix breakfast for her, not even put a slice of bread in the toaster. "You don't have to treat me like a guest," she said. "Just do your thing. I'll be fine." I asked her what she was going to do all day. She said she was going to get some rays and read a book without a single redeeming social value.

"You're not fed up with your job, are you?" I said. I couldn't, myself, imagine writing about lip gloss and acne cream all day without slipping into a self-loathing mode.

"I don't know what I am," Beth said, and I got the sense that her uneasiness had everything to do with Andy's leaving her; she was suffering from prefeminist abandonment syndrome. "Maybe I'll like go make a shitload of money somewhere," she said. "I've got the credentials."

I told her that I was going to take Marshall for a beach walk before I started working and that she knew where everything was, didn't she?

"Mom, please, just go."

I grabbed a jacket and went down to the beach. Coming abreast of the Brenner house, I saw the yellow tape fluttering slightly in the breeze. The house seemed empty; it's odd, but you can tell when a house is unoccupied, just as you can sense when you're being stared at. I started up the wooden staircase and when I reached the top, I spotted a Truro police car on the land side of the house. A barely nubile cop was sitting in the driver's seat, reading a newspaper. He saw me before I had a chance to leave, unnoticed. He got slowly out of the car and stood looking at me across the top of the Ford Crown Victoria.

"Hi there," he said. "What can I do for you?"

"Nothing, really," I said. "I live just a little ways down the beach. I was curious about what happened here yesterday."

"They don't tell me that much," he said. "But I do know this creepy guy from off-Cape splashed red paint all over this new house."

I asked him if they had caught the guy.

"He got away," the cop said. "Would you like a doughnut?"

I shook my head. "But thanks."

"I probably shouldn't be telling you this, but you know Corn Hill?"

I nodded.

"Well, a couple of weeks ago it was Wednesday, no Thursday, I know because that's the day I got early shift and they sent me up to the Corn Hill parking lot to check it out. Somebody put these flyers on some cars left overnight. They said, like BEWARE! DON'T LET THE JEWS TAKE OVER

76

TRURO. Something like that."

"My God," I said. "Do they know who did that?"

"Uh-uh."

I asked him if he knew where Mrs. Brenner was. He didn't know that either. He was not exactly bursting with information.

Just then a piece of electronic equipment started crackling inside the car. "Gotta get that," he said, and ducked inside.

I turned to leave. Nice kid.

As I walked back to my house, troubled by what I'd heard, I was sorry I hadn't accepted the doughnut.

The police were now certain that Raymie's erstwhile guest was the perpetrator. They were also thinking of charging him with attempted murder. But they had no hard evidence, as he had successfully covered both his previous and current tracks, making an efficient getaway, presumably off the Cape and into the great American landscape beyond. I wondered why he had chosen Truro in which to activate his spleen — I know, firsthand, similar monstrosities in easier places to get to and away from, like Chestnut Hill, Massachusetts, and on the North Shore. Actually, they're all over the affluence map. Sometimes what the new owner of a perfectly fine house does is tear it down and build another twice or three times as large on the same modest lot. They look as if someone had tried to squeeze a fat woman into a dress two sizes too small for her.

The phone lines from Hyannis to the tip of Provincetown were abuzz. Everyone was talking to everyone else about the vandalism and the anti-Semitism, and don't think for a minute that an awful lot of people didn't say the Brenners deserved it for violating the Lower Cape unpretentiousness code, predicting it would happen again, and furthermore they hoped whoever did it would escape punishment permanently — and hopefully go on to rid the landscape of the big-house blight. People felt that strongly.

On Sunday, Justin Sheed, a popular, occasionally retro minister in Wellfleet, arose before his Protestant flock and delivered a sermon on the perils of excess and the almost biblical aphorism "What goes around comes around." He instructed the congregation to remember Terence's advice — "moderation in all things" — and advised them to resist the temptation to "acquire mindlessly at the expense of virtue," stopping just short of saying the owners of the besmirched house deserved what they got. This sermon caused a sensation. All the local papers covered it and the *Boston Globe* sent a reporter down to sniff out some of the gamier facts. She arrived at my front door — "Hi, I'm Megan Solomon" — at ten in the morning two days after the incident, having called me first to ask if I would see her. "You're the closest neighbor," she told me, at which I twitched with pleasure — someone wanted to interview me! I offered her a drink, which she declined. "I'm all set," she said.

Megan looked younger than Beth, who sat down with us and I think had a hard time letting me answer Megan's questions. Most of these dealt with what she called "issues" (When had problems become issues? About the same time houses became homes) in Truro and the surrounding area. How did we feel about new people coming in and building houses as big as the Brenners'? Had I ever come across anti-Semitism in Truro? She had pushed the right button, and I took off with opinions that had been shaped and hardened over the past few years. She was writing a lot of what I told her in a notebook while keeping an eye on the small, pricey tape recorder she'd brought with her and which presumably was whirring away, recording my words for the ages. She asked me about the Tinkham murder. "There's absolutely no connection," I said, sensing the direction she was pointing: Truro — trouble in paradise. I tried to assure her that crime was almost unknown here — the police have nothing more to do than look out for windows blown open in the winter when the summer folks have gone back to wherever they came from. "You'll have to admit that two incidents in so short a time indicates something," Megan said.

"Well yes," I said. "But that's just a coincidence." Her eyebrows shot up.

Beth said, "We don't lock our doors . . ."

"Is that so?" Megan said. "Is that going to change, do you think?"

"Absolutely not," I told her.

"I'll have that iced tea now," she said.

Megan stayed for lunch — tuna fish sandwiches and one of my quickie cold soups. It turned out that she and Beth had friends in common, people who they started babbling about. Well, this was going swimmingly and maybe she would soften her attitude toward the very rich.

When Megan Solomon's piece appeared later that same week, my fears were realized. "The majority of the residents of Truro, a small, isolated rural community — it boasts neither supermarket, gas station, nor community center, not to mention bar and grill — seem to think that, because they are ecologically virtuous, they are immune to the ills that plague modern society, things like greed, corruption and violence. And so they were awoken with a start last week when an ecoterrorist, a man who calls himself Lyle Halliday, a clever and elusive individual, allegedly poured fake blood all over a new house and left a hate message behind." Solomon's piece touched on the unsolved murder as well, implying that the Truro police had demonstrated not even minimum competence. She had interviewed a dozen people, all the way from the one member of the Tinkham family willing — and stupid enough — to talk to a reporter, to the owner of the biggest and noisiest gay bar in P'Town, to the owner of the in-crowd's restaurant in Wellfleet, to the owner of the place with the swimming pool, to just regular folks — including me. She got people not only to talk but to blab. She was very good — cheeky behind a reticent exterior.

Solomon's article didn't bother me the way it bothered some — Molly, for instance, who wondered how this green kid could come out here and get the whole picture in forty-eight hours. "I've lived here for fifteen years and I still know squat about what really goes on." Even Raymie grumbled. "She was a little hard on us. I mean as far as most communities go, I know we're not exactly the model of virtue, but we're hardly the most morally dense either."

I said I thought Solomon had done what she came here to do. "She had an agenda. On the other hand," I told her, you couldn't discount how much satisfaction it gave certain people to dump on trophy houses — or alternatively, "McMonsters." These folks were venomous. And do you know what was so odd about the situation? That people like Mitch Brenner thought the rest of us were envious of him and his hideous house. I worried there was nothing to compare this to. Then I realized I was wrong — there was: "You know how you said you don't want to wear anything that has somebody else's name on it, not even an alligator. But the people who pay big bucks for a Coach bag or a Burberry — they think they're the cat's pajamas — not the clothes, but themselves. They think we're all dying to wear the same crap they are and the only reason we don't is that we can't afford to. Personally, I'd rather stick pins in my eyeballs."

Things sped up. The trail Lyle Halliday left behind grew faint and fainter, like an ink drawing left out in the rain. No bloodhounds, the Truro and Provincetown police did not have the equipment — technical or cerebral — to follow it and Halliday lost himself somewhere in the great landscape of the United States. The *Cape Cod Times* twitted the authorities for losing him without a fight, day after day, sometimes in a feature, sometimes an editorial, and most awfully, a cartoon showing cops in the Truro dump, kicking pretzel-shaped beach chairs and broken pottery with clumsy boots: "leaving no stone unturned in the Halliday investigation." The police's response to the Halliday vandalism was compared and contrasted ad nauseam to the Tinkham murder, not only still unsolved but yellowing with age. It was really an exercise in self-loathing because, after all, we were one of only three or four remaining nearly crime-free areas in the country. What struck me and my friends — Molly, Raymie, the ladies at the Truro Historical Society where I volunteered once a week, and my irregular lunch group — as far more important than the crime rate was the rate at which the McMonsters were being erected.

Beth — whose imagination is even livelier than mine — said she believed a bunch of aliens had landed on Earth and, bringing with them their own construction crews, put these big houses strategically over the sweetest terrain on the East Coast, and when it came time, they would swoop down on us, carry us to their domains and make us their slaves. I asked her when she thought that time would be. She didn't have any idea. "But doesn't it seem odd to you that five years ago there weren't any trophy houses and now there are dozens?"

Not odd at all. Instead of trickling down, money was defying gravity and dripping up into the hands of people who had never had much, if any, before and, I said, "I probably shouldn't be saying this out loud, but they haven't the foggiest idea what constitutes good taste."

Beth said she didn't know why that was such an awful thing to say.

I sat down and began to draw my version of the perfect trophy house. Vaguely but insincerely Italianate in style, with compulsive symmetry, a double-staircase entry, with plant-bearing urns on either side of the entrance. The door was wide enough to drive a Hummer through and the roof sloped not ungracefully. To break the symmetry I added a rectangular tower with a peaked roof. This went up about twenty feet beyond the roof line, more or less like that of the Brenner house. It was very wide and the number of windows suggested that inside were more rooms than even a family of five needed, not to say bathrooms galore. "Would you like me to color it?" I asked.

She nodded and I colored it tan, with a bit of blush pink. Tan all over. "Here," I said, handing her the picture, "you can have it."

It seemed to me — although it may have been wishful thinking — that Beth was slowly emerging from the fog of her breakup with Andy. I had caught her that morning with her hand on the telephone. She jumped when she saw me and moved away, so I figured she was trying to call the ex-boyfriend but was ashamed to have me know it. She said, "It's pretty good, Mom, but not awful enough. How do we know how big it is compared to the next house?"

I asked for it back and lightly sketched in an imaginary Truro beach house. The pairing reminded me of Diane Arbus' piquant photograph of the circus giant standing next to the circus midget. Beth was pleased with it. "Why don't you do a book about them?" she said.

I told her I wouldn't be able to live with the subject for the time it would take to complete it.

"Beth," I said, "how long are you going to stay here with me? Not that I wouldn't like it to be forever. I was just wondering about your job . . ."

"I don't really know." She sat in a chair that faced halfway away from me. "I loved it in the beginning. I loved seeing my name on the masthead."

I nodded, knowing the feeling. But it was Andy, she told me in the most roundabout way, who wanted her to stay at *Scrappy*. Was it the paycheck? It seemed that was a part of it. He wasn't bringing in any money, but he would graduate soon; he had been just about promised a job in one of the firms hard at work on designing a plan for Ground Zero. "An entry-level job, but it's a high-visibility place — and his uncle's one of the partners."

"That'll do it," I said. "And why not? Why not make use of every door open even just a crack? He'd be stupid not to."

"Using pull," Beth said, as if she were considering this amazing concept for the first time. "Andy's not stupid."

Again, I asked her what she had told her boss, Maria, when she'd come up here. "I saved a bunch of sick days I didn't use. Then Maria told me to take an extra few days if I needed to. She likes me, she likes my work. I guess she doesn't want me to leave. Jesus, I don't even wear lipstick. And I certainly don't put goop on my eyes. And here I am, advising these teenagers to waste their money . . ."

"Does Maria like Andy?"

"What's that got to do with anything?" Beth said. "You know what, Mom, I think you're hooked on this Andy thing." Her eyes filmed with tears. I wanted to tell her how lucky she was to be out of his clutches but, wisely, bit my tongue. Instead, I apologized and suggested we drive into town. "I'd like to see Tom," I said. Beth brightened somewhat and said she thought that was a good idea. Then she stuck it to me. "Why do you two spend so much time apart?"

This was sort of abrupt. But I guess she had every right to ask me this. It was an odd arrangement, more interesting in what it suggested than in what it really was — or so I thought at the time.

"What do you think, Beth?"

"Who cares what I think. But it's not my idea of marriage."

"I care, Beth." She turned away as it occurred to me that maybe she didn't really want to know.

"Okay, we'll go to Boston. I can miss the stop-the-Stop & Shop meeting and my lunch group. I'm tired of this place." I was lying. I almost never tire of Truro. The longer I live here, the more I admire the land and its moods. I like being here by myself and working in the quiet and the occasional wind. Beth can't understand this, but she will when she acquires some patience. It's not that I don't miss Tom, because I do, but it's not an ache the way it used to be when we were living apart; it's that I like our conversations, I like to watch his brain at work and I'm delighted that he seems to enjoy being with me. I don't even particularly mind his libertarian take on things; it's a good corrective for my going off half-cocked and always jumping to the left.

When I was in Watertown, I felt like that very rich woman they used to write about in the gossip columns who owned four houses and had a complete wardrobe stashed away in each one so she wouldn't have to bother with the business of packing each time she moved from one to the other. "I only need a teeny overnight bag," she was supposed to have said. I have two sets of art materials. So it's no big deal with my work. But the pace is different; the air isn't so clean; the noise, even on quiet Whitman Street where our house is, sounds baleful, at least to my ears; streetlights; ice on the sidewalk people are supposed to scrape and often don't; whackos muttering and gesturing as they make their way up the street; etc. If this sounds like I'm fed up with civilization, that's not far off the mark. If I thought human beings had managed to pull them-selves out of the muck of primitive exis-tence and its violence, bestiality, cruelty, and sloth, then maybe I wouldn't mind it so much.

But at least I could walk around the corner and buy some of the Middle Eastern food I love.

CHAPTER 4

I gathered a few of my more presentable clothes — pants with a visible crease, a couple of sweaters and shirts, a pair of real shoes, along with most of the perishable food, and deposited them haphazardly in the trunk of the Saab with its seven Truro stickers. We headed toward Boston on Route 6. It's not the most eye-catching stretch of highway; in fact, it's boring, having few vistas and little to break the wall of heavy trees on either side of the road, a good many of them infected with some sort of crinkly brown blight. I had a subdued Beth for company; along about Sandwich she stuck those little black things in her ears and listened to a CD that reached my own ears as a high whistle. She had that slightly queasy look that suggested she was thinking about Andy, on whom, in spite of the facts, she had turned a rosy light. You can't say it often enough: people believe what they want to believe, no matter how weighty the evidence against doing so.

There wasn't, thank God, much traffic

on a weekday in mid-September. The usual plumbers' and contractors' vans, a few SUVs crammed with junk not to be used until next summer. As we approached Sandwich and the Sagamore Bridge, my heart did its familiar dip of resignation. I hated crossing that bridge and returning to a life that in many respects was easier and more convenient — food shopping, nearby dry cleaner, drugstore and post office within easy walking distance, and friends to have lunch with. But somehow the convenience had a stifling effect on me. Living in Watertown meant a dozen decisions a day rather than two or three, and an urban landscape interchangeable with any fairly prosperous middle-class city in the U.S. I don't want to sound like Thoreau, because as far as I'm concerned he was a self-righteous prig: I'm more spiritual than you are because I own only one tin cup and a pencil I made myself. My Truro life isn't about being spiritual — whatever that means — but about not having "things" and commitments pressing against you all the time. On the Cape I have my work and my meals, a few protest meetings to keep me on my toes, and my trusty telephone lifeline. My existence there is spare but hardly primitive: I seem not to want any-

91

thing — that is, any material objects — beyond what I already have.

We got stuck, bumper-to-bumper, as the Boston skyline loomed. The so-called Big Dig, a sweeping abstract notion, animated, that involved removing a long stretch of elevated highway while not disturbing traffic coming and going, had, for the past five years, jammed cars together just when they most needed to hurry. We put up with it mostly in silence, counting on the powers that be to do it right while it costs taxpayers huge bucks and opens itself up to continual claims of mismanagement and fraud. Typical city troubles.

I had to pee and there was nothing to do but sit in the car stoically and wait while the traffic jam slowly, so slowly, sorted itself out. Beth said, surprising the hell out of me, "I'm thinking of quitting my job."

I asked her why, while trying not to sound happy about it.

"The things I do are so unmeaningful. Lipstick, eye shadow, fasting for your figure. Should you have cosmetic surgery or Botox at sixteen, or should you wait until you're twenty-one? It's disgusting. If you don't look like Britney Spears or a rock star, you might as well throw yourself over the nearest cliff. I'm not doing them any favors."

"You're beginning to sound like me."

I could look over at her because we weren't moving. I saw on her face an expression I hadn't seen before — a look that means I know you're right and I thank you for the compliment but I'm certainly not going to admit it.

I asked her what she thought she might do and where she intended to live. I was surprised to hear that she had some "leads" to work in the Boston area, which meant she had actually begun to plan for a future without Andy. "I thought I'd find a place somewhere like Jamaica Plain or Charlestown. I've got friends both those places — they're looking around for me. Or I might move in with one of them."

The line of cars started up again and eventually we reached the Mass. Turnpike, paid fifty cents to leave it, skirted Cambridge and drove up Mt. Auburn Street to Watertown. The trip door-to-door took just over three hours; it should take just over two.

It was afternoon when we drove into our driveway and unpacked the car, making several trips from trunk to front door. The answering machine was beeping. Our house was a nice old place, built around 1910, with blondish floors and colorful

area rugs, a lot of light, and furniture reflective of maybe four different decades,
beginning in the sixties. Tom and I had
done the so-called decorating together,
long before, when we got along so well a
look from one of us to the other said as
much as an entire act from a long play. A
friend of ours, visiting for the first time
and expecting glamour, told us, "You
people live like graduate students." He
didn't mean it as a compliment, but that's
how I took it. I hate when everything
matches perfectly, when it looks like a
room in a spec house.

I asked Beth to find out who had called,
while I stored our food and tried to decide
whether or not we had to do some food
shopping or could make do with what we
had.

"It was Dad," Beth told me. "He won't
be home for dinner. A meeting or something . . ."

"Oh?" I said. The day before, he had
told me that he would be home in time for
dinner. I phoned his office and there was
no one there; I left a message saying that
I'd got his message and couldn't wait to
see him. At least I wouldn't have to go to
the market until the next day.

Beth and I ate dinner around the corner

at the Town Diner, a Watertown fixture featuring things like a Middle Eastern platter and old-fashioned meatloaf. When we got back, around eight, Tom was still not home. Beth remarked on it, without inflection, just something about her father's changing his habits. I watched a stupid television show, until I heard Tom's key in the front door, heard the front door close with a soft thud. "Anybody home?"

I went out to the foyer. Tom was standing inside the front door with his barn jacket still on, looking somewhat baffled, as if he weren't sure he'd stepped into the right house.

"Hi, Dannie," he said, and started to take off the jacket.

I went up to him and hugged him. "I'm so glad you're here."

"Me too," he said. He rubbed the back of my head.

I asked him if he'd eaten and he nodded. "I had a bite in the student cafeteria." I asked him what the meeting was about. The usual damn thing, he told me, namely how to dole out beginning courses among senior faculty. "Someone always wants it to be 'fair.'"

"You're not one of them, I suppose," I said.

"Sometimes yes, sometimes no. I'm beat;

I can't think of anything right now except a good night's sleep."

By the time I had taken a shower and put on my pajamas, Tom was asleep on his back, snoring softly. I kissed his cheek but he didn't stir. I had a very hard time falling asleep — I usually have insomnia the first few nights in a different bed. I finally fell asleep around 2 a.m. and by the time I opened my eyes again, it was eight-thirty and the man of the house had already left. I found a note on the kitchen counter next to the butter, which he had neglected, as usual, to put back in the refrigerator. There were toast crumbs to sweep into my hand and deposit in the convenient Insinkerator (what a name!). I have a view over the kitchen sink: the house next door, a brown-stained wooden structure of no particular distinction with a kitchen window approximately opposite ours. Sometimes I see my neighbor, Alicia Baer, standing at her sink, doing her dishes. We wave and nod. The note said he hadn't wanted to wake me — "You looked so warm and peaceful" — but he'd see me later, after work. "I'll try to phone you later."

I assumed Beth was still asleep. I sat down at the kitchen table and ate breakfast while reading the *New York Times* (another small convenience).

Truro seemed, at this distance, on the other side of the planet. It fell, like my past, into a place where memory trumped everything else. I phoned Raymie to let her know I was in Watertown.

"You'll never guess where I went yesterday."

"I haven't a clue."

"I went to see Mitch Brenner in the hospital."

"You *what?*"

"I visited your neighbor. He's in Cape Cod Hospital. He's still in traction."

I listened to details of legs broken and rebroken, minor kidney problems, a touch of pneumonia. And where was the wife? Ruthie had taken a hike when it became apparent that she would have to be a full-time nurse for several months at least and would be bathing him instead of partying with him. He was understandably bitter about this and called her an assortment of unflattering names. Raymie agreed. "That's what you get when you marry a trophy wife. Only in health, never in sickness. First sign of an ugly rash and I'm out of here."

But what had induced her to visit the

enemy? Well, she'd heard about Ruthie's defection and felt sorry for him. I was so nonplussed by this news that I had a hard time responding, and trying to figure out exactly what I thought.

Raymie went blithely on. She had found him almost pathetically grateful for her visit; it seemed that she was only one of very few people willing to travel from wherever they lived all the way to Hyannis. Some had sent flowers instead and his private room was crammed with them, several of them wilting on their stems. "He's not so awful, really," she said. "He was nice to the nurse."

"That's a terrific sign," I said, wondering how he behaved when no one was looking.

He and Raymie had had a wonderful visit. "He really loves the Cape," she said, even though there was no nightlife to speak of and you had to create your own pleasures. He had offered her Italian chocolates his son had sent him. The son lived in Boulder. He hadn't come to see his father, since the injuries weren't life-threatening. And what about his daughter? She lived in Switzerland and she wasn't about to come either. Although still on painkillers, Mitch was fixated on catching the person who had vandalized his house. He referred to him as a terrorist.

I thought that was something of an exaggeration, but I suppose that when someone pours blood on your house without even making your acquaintance first, you're apt to lose a sense of proportion. I asked her how long she had stayed.

"Well," she said, "I drove more than an hour to get there; I wasn't about to turn around and come right back. A couple of hours, I guess. I'm going again next week."

"You're not," I said. It just popped out.

"What's the matter, Dannie? Why shouldn't I? Here's this guy, he'll never walk right again, someone desecrated his house, his family are all shits, and I feel good about making him less miserable. I'd like to know what's wrong with that?"

I asked her why she was being so defensive, not exactly the most tactful response, and Raymie bristled. This was the first time, she said, that she ever heard of someone being ragged on for showing compassion. And I suppose she had a point. Pity had never been Raymie's strongest point. Not that she didn't have any but that other traits came first: imagination, humor, intelligence, warmth.

"Well," I said, "when you go back, say hello for me." I was uncharacteristically baffled. What did Raymie have in mind?

My workroom was on the third floor of our house, once a dusty attic. It has a sloping ceiling and a skylight cut into the roof over the spot where I work. My art things were where I had left them months earlier, carefully, if not compulsively cleaned, lined up, boxed, stacked, accounted for, the wastebasket empty, the cupboard latched. It looked as if a good person worked here, an orderly person. I started on a new project. My favorite children's book editor, David Lipsett, a man with a seriously sexy voice, whom I had never met, kept sending me work, one book after another. I lost myself in time, thinking of nothing but story and shape and color. I worked until the phone rang. It was Tom, asking if I'd like to go somewhere nice for dinner. We discussed the relative pluses and minuses of various places to eat and settled on one in Cambridge, in Harvard Square, that he seemed to know quite well — that is, he reeled off some of the items on the menu and said it was a nice, quiet restaurant: you could hear yourself think. I realized, really for the first time, that, not a particularly good and certainly not an ardent cook, Tom must eat out quite often whenever I was on the

Cape and he wasn't. I pictured him at a table alone, with an open book propped against the bread basket, eating simply and maybe not noticing that they had brought him spinach salad and not the garden greens he had ordered. It made me feel sorry for him, wanting to talk to someone about his research or a paper he was writing or even engage in the kind of small talk that happens over a meal. We agreed to meet at seven. Beth was still living in the house, but she had given me and her father instructions not to ask her any questions that began with the word "when." She also said that I should assume she would not be home for dinner unless she told me otherwise. It was obvious that she was uneasy about the ties that bind getting tighter and tighter until she could no longer breathe.

When I got to the restaurant, Tom hadn't yet shown up. The headwaiter led me to our table, set for four. I ordered a glass of the house wine, sipping it while I studied the menu, choosing silently. Then I looked up and saw Tom and a man I didn't recognize. Tom leaned over and kissed my cheek. "You look nice," he said. "Very healthy." He introduced the man as Doug Herbert. "Doug's just joined the department." I wondered why Tom hadn't told me about our third wheel. He was perfectly pleasant but basically bland. He didn't get the point of a joke Tom told and had to have it explained. Then he told us about his new Toyota and all the high-tech stuff in it. When I asked him where he lived, he gave me the long answer: a condo with a slice of a view of the Charles River, a laundry in the basement, "superior" security, central AC and a parking place reserved for himself. I caught Tom's eye and read his message back to me: "Sorry." Holding up a dinner-table conversation with this man was as exhausting as carrying a heavy toddler up three flights of stairs. My mood began to shift and I found myself hating Douglas Herbert and blaming him for my falling spirits.

Tom ordered dessert, then espressos, and by the time he'd paid the bill and set Herbert free into the Cambridge night, I was far from sanguine. We got into the Saab in silence. Tom let me drive.

"Is something wrong?" I said.

"Nothing's wrong. Why do you ask?"

"I mean this is the first time we've been alone since I got back."

"We were alone last night," Tom said. "How's the car behaving?"

"It's fine. I love it," I said. "For five

minutes. We were alone."

"I was really beat," he said.

"What's with this guy you brought along to dinner?" The lights were out in most of the houses we drove past. It's a sleepy part of the world.

"Doug? He just joined the department," Tom said, using the exact words he'd used earlier. "Just went through a divorce. Apparently not the amicable kind. I thought I'd be kind for once and invite the poor guy to join us. He knows hardly anybody in Cambridge."

"Why do you say that? You're kind a lot of the time," I told him.

"If you say so," Tom said. "The light's green."

I was uncomfortable, my food backing up slightly. I asked Tom for my Rolaids. "They're in my purse." He plunged his fingers into the bag, looking as if he weren't sure a family of mice hadn't made a nest inside it. "What's all this junk?" he said. "Do you have indigestion?"

"Just a touch," I said. "The duck was too rich."

By the time I had caught Tom up on Beth's news and my own — what there was of it — we had reached our house. "It's sort of nice to be back," I said.

"Shall we celebrate your return?" he said somewhat archly. He meant we should make love. So we did and it was okay, though in the middle of it I found myself thinking about our odd dinner and afterward was afraid to ask Tom what he was thinking about. Within a minute or two Tom was asleep and I figured I might as well visit dreamland myself.

The next morning Tom was cheerful. Sex does have a way of making the air brighter. He went off to work, kissing me on the cheek and telling me how nice it was for him to have me home.

As always, I had work to do. I went to the third floor and applied myself to the job, with a small radio tuned to WGBH — they play nothing but classical music until late in the afternoon. They were doing Mozart's *Requiem*, which makes my heart bleed.

I worked until some time after noon, when I realized I was too hungry to concentrate. As soon as I opened the refrigerator door, the phone rang. It was David Lipsett, the editor of the book I had been struggling to illustrate. I wasn't pleased with my efforts because the book was another helping of Cream of Wheat. I complained to David and he said, "That's the last of her," meaning the author. "We had a contractual obligation." Then he told me he'd called to find out how I was doing. "I see you're back in Watertown," he said.

I told him I'd moved back for the winter. He asked about "the family." He said the air downtown was still loaded with particulates; his secretary had suddenly developed asthma. "She's a middle-aged woman. She can hardly breathe." He seemed to want to linger on the phone. I asked him whether he thought one of his books might be right for photographs instead of hand-done artwork. "I didn't know you were a photographer too," he said. Then he suggested that I show him some of my work. "I'd have to come along with it," I said.

"That sounds fine," he said. "I'd like to see what you look like after all these years."

"I haven't been to New York in a couple of years."

"It's changed a lot since you were here last," he said. "It's about time you paid it a visit. It's perfectly safe, you know — all things considered. And I'd really like to see your work." I could have said that I thought those things considered were considerable and that his secretary's health problem was the least of it. But I didn't say anything. He kept me on the phone until I'd promised to let him know when I planned to come.

I made myself a salad of mostly leftover vegetables and ate it while doing the *Times* crossword puzzle. The salad didn't do the trick and I went back for peanut butter.

New York. Where would I stay? I had a cousin, Caroline, a woman I rarely saw but whose Christmas cards always included an invitation to "stay with us when you come to the Big Apple." Her husband was a congenital grouch. But the idea of going to New York appealed to me. No, more than that. I was excited, although it wouldn't do to let David Lipsett know how eager I was to accept his invitation. I knew next to nothing about him, whether he was married, nor whether he was straight or gay. It was never safe to draw premature conclusions about a New Yorker, especially if he was in publishing.

That afternoon I took the bus to Harvard Square, where I dropped off some of my best photographs at Ferranti-Dege to be enlarged: a couple of twiggy dunes at dusk, one of Raymie at her stove, perspiring, one of Marshall looking dumb and troubled, one of Provincetown Harbor from half a mile away and a couple of others — an assortment I figured would show my range and depth. I felt about eighteen years old, which says something about how my expectations had, over the past several years, grown flat, flattened, how the line of my life had so few dips and rises that I might as well have been lying comatose in some intensive care unit. Conversely, the anticipation of a solo visit to the most exciting city in the world was as heady as a couple of strong drinks. It was almost as if the last thirty-plus years had never happened.

I inspected my closet. Most of my clothes went back to the eighties; I couldn't seem to get rid of them. A couple of things were quaintly out of fashion while others had, inexplicably, shrunk. What did they wear in New York? Black. Black for work, black for a party. Black for grocery shopping and a dentist appointment. Did they wear black nightgowns and panties as well? I had one pair of halfway decent black wool crepe pants and an off-white silk blouse. But no jacket I would be caught dead in. I drove over to the Watertown Mall, not your most upscale emporium, but a place where you could find a bargain if you knew what you were looking for. I bought a black linen jacket. It had been almost a year since I had bought anything new besides a bathing suit and a pair of hideous gray walking shoes with wraparound rubber soles and long white laces that dragged on the ground. Beth teases me about how little money I spend on myself. It's true, but why bother when you're alone so much of the time? And when Tom was with me, did he notice?

The next time I talked to Raymie, she had just come back from the hospital where Mitchell Brenner was rehabbing. She was almost giddy. "We had him all wrong," she said. "He's really a pussycat." I couldn't match this appraisal with the Mitch Brenner I knew. But I wasn't stupid enough to believe that a person always wears the same face, no matter who he's with or how he feels. Smarmy to his superiors, pissy to the flight attendant. But still, I was sure this man was bone-deep arrogant and foolish. Beth would have said "asshole."

"I don't quite see that, Raymie," I said.

"Well, you two must have got off on the wrong foot." I reminded her that she had seen him first, at Caro's, when he bribed the headwaiter for the Mailers' table. He wasn't a pussycat then, was he? She didn't answer.

"What about his house?" I asked. Had they found Halliday?

Fed up with the Truro police, Mitch had hired a P.I. to track the vandal. "It's costing him big bucks," she said, "but he wants to nail this guy. So do I, for that matter. They think he's still on the East Coast."

"By the way," I said. "Why did he write 'Jew Pig' if Mitch isn't Jewish?"

"Mitch *is* Jewish," Raymie said. "Though you wouldn't know it by anything he does or says. He doesn't talk about it. He's very skeptical about religion in general. He hates Baptists the most."

"Well," I said. "Who cares as long as he's good to his girlfriend? And if Halliday's looking to do it again, there are plenty of trophy houses in the area, though so far, thank God, none in Watertown."

I guess Raymie figured it was about time to drop her bombshell: Mitch had asked her to move in with him as soon as the kitchen was up and running. She had agreed.

"You're going to live there?" Had she gone round the bend?

"He needs someone to look after him."

"Oh, he's going to pay you?"

"He offered to, but I told him I didn't need a salary."

Didn't need a salary? What was she thinking of? If she gave up her B&B and went to live in the monster house with the monster and then something happened, say he got tired of her and kicked her out, where would she go? How would she live? Whatever it was that made her take this sudden turn in her life, the future didn't seem to matter to her as much as it did the rest of us.

While all this was going on inside my head, Raymie clarified her role: "Call me a companion," she said. "He's going to need a lot of help around this house. And you know what a fabulous cook I am." Should I tell Raymie what I thought about this scheme? She hadn't asked me, but it was easy to see that she didn't want to hear anything except approval. Deciding to keep my thoughts to myself, I asked what she was going to do with her bed-and-breakfast.

"How would you like to take it over?" she said. "Just kidding."

Mark came over for dinner. Beth stayed in to join us. Tom was in one of his better moods; he likes having his children around. The four of us hadn't sat down together for a meal in a long time. Mark was characteristically vague about his future; he and Beth built a fantasy about the two of them running a ski-boarding school — something neither of them knew how to do — along with a jazz bar nestled somewhere in the Rocky Mountains. Here were two adults with no more idea of what they would be doing in five years than Marshall did. And this didn't seem to bother them in the least. It would have driven me nuts — but I was born in 1950, when certainty ranked high and footloose was taboo — except for the beatniks who practically invented it. But it makes a mother feel warm all over to see her children get along so well together.

After Mark left and Beth went to her room, Tom mentioned that his department was going to give a small party for the new man in town. "We're inviting significant others," Tom said. "Do you want to come?"

"You know how I love those events," I said. "The laity all stand together and talk about local real estate, and day care, and, if they're really hard up for a topic, the weather, while you guys huddle and talk shop. The food is squares of white American cheese on toothpicks and crescents of mushy apple. The wine is so-so and —"

"Then don't come," he said, interrupting me.

"I'm sorry," I said. I'd hurt his feelings. I don't know why I do things like that. "Of course I'll come. When is it?"

"Friday," he said. "Five o'clock."

The party turned out to be less parochial than others I'd been to. In the first place, it was held in the Faculty Club, high above sea level, with a glowing view of the Boston skyline, beyond the Charles River, thousands of lights twinkling behind apartment and office windows. In the second, they served real booze and real hors d'oeuvres — triangular spinach pies, stuffed mushrooms, catered items like that. I figured MIT was having a fat year, based, no doubt, on spectacular antiterrorism devices. Not for nothing was the place known as the Military Institute of Technology. The women were dressed up — at least for Cambridge, which meant no jeans or sneakers. I wore my new jacket, which Tom didn't recognize as new but I let it pass. I began to have a passively good time, talking to a couple of faculty wives — Jean, Greta — not about real estate but about their work — and mine. Jean wanted to tell Greta about the Tinkham murder (which everyone seemed to know about) and the vandalism. I told her it was a neighbor's house, not quite finished. She made me describe the house. I sort of embroidered the damage, but as I spoke, I was drawn backward in time and realized how agitated I had been when it happened.

"Who's that woman?" I asked, pointing my chin in the direction of Tom, where he was chatting it up with a woman about my age, maybe a little younger but not much, in a smart gray skirt suit and black pumps. She was looking at him as if he was telling her something supremely fascinating, something that no one else had any inkling of, something that would change her life from blue to red, from tiny to huge, from dull to sparkling.

"The one with the great skin?" Jean said. "That's Judith Levy. She's on a Knight Fellowship — they're science writers. MIT brings them here for a year and lets them sample the assorted academic wares. If you ask me, she seems to be devoting an awful lot of time to anthropology."

I looked hard at Judith Levy. Even across the room you could tell she had that kind of silken skin that converts an ordinary-looking woman into a stunner. It seems to be infused with its own natural makeup, pale and creamy, soft as a butterfly. "She does have a fairly nice complexion," I said. "Excuse me, I think I'll go over and meet her." As I said this, I caught a look that passed from Jean to Greta and back. I wanted to tell them to get a life but I kept my mouth shut.

On the way over, I stopped at the bar and ordered a whiskey and water, from which heat. It heated my chest.

"Hi, Dannie," Tom said. "Having a good time?"

"I'm having a very nice time, thank you." I stuck my hand toward Judith Levy's midsection. "I'm his wife," I said. She told me she was pleased to meet me as the color of her cheeks deepened to a dark pink. I looked for a wedding ring. No wedding ring, though she wore a rather large and showy star sapphire on her right third finger. Tom introduced us. He told me Judith had been auditing one of his courses, then decided to take it for credit. "She's acing it."

"How nice," I said. I felt like a Meg Ryan character — assailable, slightly addled — while trying not to let my confusion show. I asked Judith a string of polite questions: What had she done in Boston? What sort of science writing did she do? Tom kept nodding as she answered.

I decided that Judith Levy was far too anxious to earn an A from Tom. I hate people like that. They're so damn transparent. I drank another whiskey and probably shouldn't have driven home by myself. But I made it without anything untoward happening.

I was in the kitchen, heating some leftover bean soup, when Tom came into the kitchen. "Nice party," I said.

"I thought so too," he said. He opened the refrigerator and stuck his head inside. "Is Beth here?"

I told him she wasn't. He emerged with a thick wedge of cheddar. Then he looked for something to eat it on top of. Men never know where anything is in the kitchen.

"Where's that bread?"

"Which bread is that?"

"What's the matter with you, Dannie? Did I do something wrong?"

"I just can't believe you let that woman brown-nose you that way . . ."

"Oh, for Pete's sake, Dannie, leave the poor woman alone. She's working very hard. It's not an easy course. Lots of statistics."

I could have pursued this line but decided not to, though I couldn't have said why. "Guess what Raymie's going to do?"

He found the bread in the bread box and pounced on it, waving it in front of me as if he'd discovered Atlantis. Subtext: I had deliberately hidden it from him. "Raymie?" he said. "What's the old girl up to now?"

"She's going to move in with our neighbor, Mitchell Brenner."

"She's a fool." He stuffed his mouth with food and began to chew it.

Beth came home before he had swallowed. "Were you two out somewhere?" Without waiting for an answer, she told us she'd got an apartment in Jamaica Plain with one of her friends. "It's got two bedrooms and it's a block from the Pond. They just did the kitchen over."

"That's great, Beth," Tom said. "How are you going to pay the rent?"

"I'm temping at John Hancock 'til I find something I really want to do."

"What happened to your plan to go back to New York?"

"I'm going to wait. Maybe in a year or so. Anyway, I like being near you guys and Mark."

This was gratifying but I knew it was only partly true. She couldn't face New York without Andrew. She shouldn't let him continue to determine the direction or shape of her life. This was like one of your basic stories: "From beyond the grave his evil influence continues to hold sway over the brokenhearted maiden." Except Andy wasn't dead. Maybe I'd just kill him.

"I'm beat," Tom said. "I'm going to bed."

CHAPTER 5

I invited my neighbor, Alicia Baer, for coffee on the morning before I left for New York. What I had in mind was for her to let Marshall out into the backyard a couple of times a day and walk him if and when Tom hadn't come home by seven. This was something she'd done for me in the past. I felt a little guilty asking her, but she seemed agreeable enough; I always brought back a small thank-you gift for her. Alicia's married to a surgeon named Barney, who has this habit of turning a fishy stare on you, as if he were trying to decide where to make the first incision. Alicia is in her sixties and is an editor, semiretired, in an ancient Boston publishing house. That day, as soon as she sat down at the counter in my kitchen, she remarked that I looked especially "bright and bushy-tailed." I took this to mean that my excitement had broken through onto my cheeks and lit up my eyes. "How long since you've been to New York?" Alicia asked.

"Three or four years, I guess," I said. "I

really have no reason to go."

"No exhibits? No galleries? No friends?"

"I suppose I ought to," I said. "There's nothing to stop me."

What I didn't want to get into was that Tom wasn't all that high on New York and that inevitably some of his reluctance to go there had rubbed off on me; I didn't want to appear to be buying into my husband's opinions wholesale. New York, he insisted, was noisy, crowded, dirty, unsafe — even before September 11. It was expensive; risk lurked everywhere from the cabdriver who tried to stiff you to the maid in the hotel who probably went through your things. He admitted he found it exciting at night. The lights and the constant buzz of people having — or trying to have — a good time, was, as he called it, infectious. Usually, when we went there together, he took the West Side subway to Columbia to see his pals and colleagues while I visited galleries and shoe stores.

I had known Alicia for more than ten years, so I was surprised when she now told me that she had, more than twenty years earlier, almost split with her husband and gone to New York to take a fabulous job in a classy publishing house. "Trying to decide whether or not to leave here was

118

one of the most awful periods of my whole life; I think I actually may have gone a little nuts. I wouldn't want to go through that again."

"How did you decide?" I said. "I hope you don't mind my being nosy."

She brushed this off, saying she didn't consider me the least bit nosy. "I guess I just tried to measure the potential pain of leaving my husband against missing out on a great career move. The trouble was, of course, that since both were in the future, how could I do this? Either one would have to be just a guess."

"Can I ask you a question? And if you don't want to answer, I wouldn't blame you," I said. "Please don't feel you owe me an answer."

Alicia told me not to worry. Beating around the bush was not her style.

And so I asked her if she regretted the choice she'd made. And she said, surprisingly, "Sometimes."

But why should that surprise me? No human being on earth reaches fifty without dragging behind them at least a few regrets. If there are folks out there free of this baggage, I'd very much like to meet them, although they're probably unbearably smug. I, for one, regret that I didn't let my high school sweetheart, Barry Chang, make love to me. He was the most adorable boy. He played the bassoon and was an All-State track and field champion. I wanted more than anything to have sex with him; my whole body went into a meltdown whenever he touched me. But I wasn't brave enough; I still can't think of Barry without flushing. Regret stings.

"Here I am," Alicia said, "a year or so away from retirement. What do I do then to keep me busy? I don't know anything but editing. I'm not very good at keeping house, mainly because I don't really care if there are dust mice under the couch. Martha Stewart strikes me as a freak of nature — God, look what she's done to make the American woman feel inadequate. But I have Barney — he's good company when he's not seeing patients. Did I tell you, he's stopped doing surgery? He developed a slight tremor in his hands. That's it for the scalpel. But he still consults. He loves medicine the way I love publishing. So there you are. We're going to have to figure out how to give each other the most pleasure — and I'm not just talking about sex. I'm talking about enjoyment. Sounds pretty drab, doesn't it?"

I didn't think so.

"And you know what," she said, as if remembering to stick the rosebuds into the icing, "I told Barney I wish I had a spa, one of those tubs with lots of fierce nozzles and a whirlpool, in our bathroom. And of course I didn't need it, a luxurious and expensive item like that. And he urged me to go ahead and have one installed. And when I asked him why he was so easily persuaded to spend that kind of money for something so self-indulgent, you know what he said? He said, ' 'Cause it makes you happy.' " With that, Alicia looked at her watch. "I've got an eye appointment at eleven. I've got to run. Don't worry about Marshall; he'll be fine. And have fun in New York."

I took the new Amtrak Acela to New York, a smooth, almost silent ride that's supposed to shave almost an hour off the trip down the so-called Northeast corridor. However, the train mysteriously stopped outside of Bridgeport for forty-five minutes and thus took about the same time the slower train would have taken. I had decided to stay with my cousin Caroline and her husband rather than at a hotel, mainly because I experienced an unusual spurt of family loyalty — we had spent summers together as children; it might be nice to trade versions of family history. I arrived at her apartment near the U.N. complex late in the afternoon, took her and her grouchy husband out to dinner at a neighborhood restaurant, and went to bed on the early side. I thought I was too nervous to fall asleep quickly, but the opposite was true and when, the next day, I got up refreshed and went into the kitchen where Caroline was cooking bacon in the oven and brewing coffee, I was actually delighted to hear about her perfect children.

"How do I look?" I said.

"You look great — very black. Who's this person you're seeing?"

"It's a man I've been working with for years. We've never met. He's a fan of my work. He wants to see my photographs."

"Do you mind if I tell you something?"

I shook my head, certain it would be something less than lovely.

"That last book you illustrated? The one about the vegetable stand in Maryland? If you don't mind me saying so, it wasn't your best work."

I seethed and said nothing. Caroline's the person who told me, years ago, that Tom and I were ships that pass in the night. She seems to enjoy throwing darts at me — and she's got great aim. But her criticism implied she had actually looked at the book, an item meant for the under-seven crowd. Or maybe she hadn't and was lying. In any case, I suppose I shouldn't have stayed with her in the first place.

"I'll see you later," I said, looking in her hall mirror to make sure I was as snappy as I could possibly be without a total makeover. Black is good.

"Come to think of it, you could use a scarf with that outfit," Caroline said, sneaking up behind me. "Just a small touch of color at the throat."

"No thanks," I said. "I like me this way."

She made a dart into the hall closet and came out with a gauzy blue scarf that would have looked just right. "Here," she said, "it goes." I shook my head and heard her say something vaguely hissy under her breath. But I left with my pride intact and started out on foot. The throb and noise in the City always get under my skin, not in a bad way but like a powerful upper. Wings on my heels.

I walked — a matter of a mile or so — to the building in which the publishing house occupied the entire eleventh floor. I gave the man in the lobby two forms of I.D. I thought I was going to have to give over a drop or two of blood before he allowed me on the elevator. On eleven the elevator doors slid open to reveal a chrome and glass waiting room with a wall against which hung the firm's latest hits, none of them children's books. I went over to the woman sitting at a glass desk behind a glass partition and told her who I was. Soon a person in a miniskirt, looking to be about fifteen and introducing herself as Ashley, came out to collect me. "David's stuck in a meeting. He said to tell you that he'll be with you in about five minutes. I'm supposed to take you to his office and ask you if you want something to drink." I was thinking maybe a shot of whiskey to calm nerves unexpectedly jangling, but declined her offer. I followed her down a couple of corridors off which lay tiny offices containing one person each, at work. A couple of them glanced up as we passed. Hadn't he told me his assistant was middle-aged? "Are you new here?"

"I've like been here three weeks? David's old assistant had to retire. She's got lung problems. It's not cancer."

Ashley left me in her boss's office. It was just large enough for a desk, two chairs and dozens of what I assumed were manuscripts waiting to be read on the shelves against one wall. I went around to his side of the desk to look at his things. A computer, a glass paperweight, a ceramic buffalo, a fake glass pen, a picture of two small inauthentically happy children within a metal frame, along with the usual pads and memo sheets, calendar, and clock. His desktop was not especially forthcoming, if what you had in mind was revelation. It was neither messy nor compulsively neat but somewhere in between. The only thing that might have given something away was the photograph, and the subjects could be anyone — his kids, his niece and nephew, godchildren. I wondered briefly why I was being so nosy. I reminded myself: "You are not single, Dannie, and this is not a blind date. This is a man who provides you with work. Period."

"Is that Dannie?" I jumped; he'd caught me snooping at his desktop.

"Mr. Lipsett?"

"David. Please."

"David."

"Did Ashley get you something to drink?"

"I didn't want anything, thanks."

I was embarrassed, as if I'd discovered, too late, that I was wearing shoes from two different pairs.

"Well," he said as he settled himself in

the high, back-leaning leather chair on his side of the desk. "Do you have those pictures with you? Let's take a look." I noticed, as he brought his hands together, that he was missing the little finger of his right hand. This so unnerved me that I began to babble about his old assistant while trying, at the same time, to untie the black ribbon securing my portfolio. I finally got it open and laid them out for David to look at.

He examined the pictures, twelve by fifteen each, in silence, one at a time. I sat on the other side of the desk, trying not to look at the place where his finger should be and watching him for some reaction, which he maddeningly kept hidden. For a moment, it seemed more important than anything, ever, that he like them, that he tell me I was a great photographer and that, in fact, these pictures were too good for a children's book; they should have a show of their own in a gallery, later to be reproduced in a book of their own. The fantasy stopped abruptly, when he said, "They're not bad. I'll have to think about finding the right book for them. Kids like drawings, I guess because the artist takes so many liberties the photographer can't."

Was he telling me he couldn't use them?

"You can fool around with photographs,

you can do amazing things . . ."

"I know," he said. It was at this point that he smiled broadly, implying, I thought, that what I'd just said was too obvious to be put into words. "Of course you do," I said.

Meanwhile, as this back-and-forth was going on, I was studying him with far more interest than I would have admitted at the time. He was hovering in the fifty-year range, no beard or mustache, and his skin color was either Mediterranean or sun-exposed. He had on trendy, oval-shaped wire-rimmed glasses and seemed not to have lost much if any hair along the way. He was wearing a gray tweed jacket, striped shirt closed up to the highest button, no tie. His shoes were hidden but I would have bet a million dollars they didn't have tassels on them. There was a looseness to the way he moved that most women find very appealing, as if a puppeteer with not much experience was working his strings. You want to steady him. What I was trying not to admit was that I found him wickedly attractive. As I looked at this man, I formed an instant emotional opinion about him. Whether, later, I would be forced to revise or stick with a good hand, didn't figure in my calculation.

"You know," he said, tapping the pictures

together into a neat stack, "I may be able to use something of yours — not necessarily any of these — in a book that's still being written, about a whale watch. You've been on one?"

I nodded. "Have you?"

"Not yet," he said. "Maybe you can tell me how it's done. I've made a reservation for lunch nearby. You're free, aren't you?"

I nodded. "Can I leave this here?" I asked, pointing to my portfolio. Only after asking did I realize that leaving it would mean I'd have to come back to retrieve it.

The restaurant was subdued, with plenty of room between tables, a maitre d' who welcomed David Lipsett by name and told him how nice it was to see him again. He led us to a banquette where we both faced out toward the other tables and diners. The light in the room was so subtle and diffused it was hard to figure out where it came from. David told me the place was popular with folks in publishing and pointed out an author whose name I recognized, sitting with his agent "rumored to be his sixth. He goes through them like popcorn."

Reluctant to make us sound like one of those magical couples in the *New York Times*' Vows column on Sundays, where every bride and every groom are so brilliant, funny, original, free of spirit, different (or "special"), I still maintain that our first conversation was nothing other than brilliant, funny, free of spirit, "special." We talked about ourselves, mostly as a means of getting the outward layers peeled away quickly. He was divorced, had been for some time. There were two children, one in college, the other in high school. "My ex and I are on pretty good terms, considering." I was glad he didn't tell me that they got on much better now that they were no longer married. (Of course people get on better after the divorce; they don't have to clean up the other person's emotional shit.) I told him, as briefly as I could, about Tom and Beth and Mark, determined to make the fantasy of being single last longer than the few hours embracing it.

I had planned to order something I had never cooked and maybe not even tasted. So I ordered a quail salad, and when I looked at the six bird corpses arranged prettily on a nest of mesclun, their legs no larger than Q-tips, I wasn't sure I wanted to eat the poor little things. David must have seen me hesitate. "We could order you something else if you don't want to eat that," he said.

"I'm going to try," I said. "Either I eat them, or they get thrown out with the coffee grounds. Do you think people working in the kitchen ever help themselves to the food left on plates?" He said he certainly hoped not but wouldn't be surprised if they did. He asked me if I'd read George Orwell's book about being a dishwasher in Paris, with roaches and rats running around the kitchen. "After I finished it," he said, "I never wanted to eat in a restaurant again. Yet here we are!" I told him I'd read the book and had had the same reaction. The funny thing was that the quail were too small to have any discernible flavor; I might as well have been eating tiny bits of anything from the bird family. We shared a pastry for dessert. By the end of the meal, when the maitre d' came over to pull out our table — and although I hadn't summoned the nerve to ask about the missing finger — I wanted to hug David and lick his ear. But I behaved myself in the manner of a married, middle-aged book illustrator who wants more work and no funny business.

"Where are you headed?" David asked as we left the restaurant.

"Back to your office," I said. "I left my portfolio there, remember?"

His cell phone sang. "Excuse me a second," he said. He talked into it, said something about a meeting at three. I looked at my watch. It was almost a quarter of three.

"Sorry about that," he said. "Life would be a lot less complicated without these contraptions. But you know, I've begun to feel naked without it."

Naked? "I'll just pick up my things and be off."

"Would you like to know what I'm thinking right now?" he said. "I'm thinking you're the most attractive woman I've ever seen."

Now I know what I look like, and while I'm quite sure no one would turn away from me in horror, I also know that compared to a truly beautiful woman — let's give her a ten — I barely make a six. My chin is a little weak, my nose a little crooked, my eyes pale rather than saturated. I should take off about fifteen pounds and strangle the gray hairs that have started to appear like weeds in a neglected lawn. Well, I thought, either he's nuts or he's smitten.

I looked down girlishly; felt girlish.

"That's a statement, Dannie," he said. "It doesn't require an answer."

With this extravagance he had jumped way over the line I myself was not prepared to cross. What did he have in mind? He had paid me one of the two compliments a woman most wants to hear, the other being "You're the smartest woman I've ever met." Did he want to tell me he liked the way I looked and leave it at that — a compliment no more significant than if he had told me he liked my shoes — or did he want to cut short the journey from cozy lunch to bed? I thanked him in a faint voice and did not turn my head to look at him.

"Jesus! Watch out!" David yelled, grabbing my arm and yanking it so hard I nearly fell over. "That kid on a bicycle almost killed you."

"What kid?" David pointed to a boy on a bicycle, wearing a black leather jacket, already halfway up the block, speeding blithely to his next delivery. David seemed more shaken than I was. Of course, he'd seen the near miss. I hadn't.

"If he'd been driving a car, I would have got his license. Damn."

"I'm fine, David, really, he missed me."

"By inches."

"That'll do it." I wanted to look cool, unconcerned, even as my heart was racing and my mouth had gone dry, while David told me about how he'd been hit by a cyclist on Seventh Avenue a few years earlier and landed in a hospital with a serious concussion. "It happened just the way it happened a minute ago," he said. "They thought I might be brain-damaged. But I was okay."

When we got back to his office, David insisted that I sit down and drink some water. He rang for Ashley, who didn't seem all that happy about being a gopher. "Where did you say you were staying?"

"Well, actually, I'm planning to take the five o'clock train back to Boston."

His four fingers and a thumb fiddled with something on his desk. "That's a pity. If you were staying another night, I'd say let's have dinner together." His suggestion, falling just short of an invitation, was so graceful that I nearly told him that I'd do it, I'd stay over and do anything that came into my head, consequences or no. I got up, gathered my things, shook hands with David, who said, "Hey, I'll walk you to the elevator."

"Thanks so much for the wonderful lunch."

"And the close call," he said.

On the train heading north I tamped

down my excitement and prepared for re-entry into the familiar. The image of David kept undercutting my best intentions. I couldn't let myself believe that I might have fallen for a near stranger. I was fifty-three; this sort of thing had gone out of my life years earlier. What the hell was I thinking?

CHAPTER 6

Beth sounded urgent and mysterious when she called to ask if she could come over to the house on Whitman Street; she had something she had to tell me. I reminded her that this was her house too. "You have a key. What's up?" She said, "I'd rather wait 'til I see you in person." She had piqued my curiosity, adding a couple of drops of anxiety. I've learned not to count on news being good.

There are dozens of me, waiting in line in the drafty building, shifting from one foot to the other, trying to read the newspaper I've brought with me without bothering the Dannie in back or in front of me. Sometimes I think I know what I'm waiting for; other times I'm baffled. When I finally reach the window, what am I going to find? Will I be told that I haven't filled out the proper forms? Will I be issued a visa for Italy or, God forbid, Afghanistan? Will I be asked to hand over a two-hundred-dollar fine for infraction of some obscure rule? Who's on the other side of the window? Waiting patiently, I am wife, mother, artist (when I allow myself this name), neighbor, home owner, food shopper, bed maker, laundress, cook, weeder, tire changer, etc., etc. But when I sense something amiss in the life of one of my children, mother empathically elbows her way to the front of the line. However muted, alarms have gone off.

So I put David Lipsett and the ecstasy I dreamed of sharing with him on hold.

"I've taken a job in New Hampshire," Beth said almost as soon as she came in through the front door.

"What kind of job?"

"It's at a sort of halfway house for kids who've been in trouble?" I wondered whether she meant halfway in or halfway out. "It's to keep them from getting worse. They've been on drugs, they've had minor scrapes with the law. Some of them are what's called 'incorrigible'?"

"You don't have any experience in that kind of work," I said, immediately regretting it.

"They're very shorthanded," she said, narrowing her eyes in a way I recognized as reflective of hurt. "They'll take almost anybody."

"Are you going to get paid for this?"

"Not quite a living wage," she said. "But housing's thrown in. So that makes up for the chintzy salary." She described the housing: a co-op arrangement, with private rooms for everyone and a common kitchen and living room. It sounded to me a bit like the halfway house the bad kids were in. It occurred to me that this might be some kind of penance she was doing, but for what? What did she think she had done that required what involved a personal sacrifice?

"Can I ask you a question?"

"You mean, am I hungry? The answer is yes."

"I'll make us something," I said, glad to be occupied in a physical task. "Sorry, I should have asked earlier. It's past lunchtime, isn't it? But that's not what I was going to ask. I was going to ask you why you're taking this job? It's not exactly your line of work."

"You think I'm going off the tracks, don't you? And it probably has something to do with Andy. But it isn't that. It's just that at the magazine I was doing such shitty work. Sometimes I felt like a slut or something. I suppose this job at Bellmont Hill — that's what the place is called — will be good for me. And maybe for the kids. I like children."

Well, I'd never heard her say this before. It might even be true. But I was skeptical of her plan. I wanted to remind her that if she wanted my approval she didn't need it and probably shouldn't be asking for it. She was thirty years old.

"You're not asking for my approval, are you?"

"Of course not. I just wanted to let you know what I'm going to do."

"You're not eating your salad," I said.

"I guess I'm not very hungry."

I decided to tell her about New York, minus the heart of the story. Beth seemed minimally interested and then told me she hoped that one day she and I could do a book together. It would be basically a picture book, with photographs of trophy houses on the Outer Cape. "You'd take the pictures," she said. "I'd do the text."

I turned the idea on its head: "How about a book of genuine Cape houses? Not even the kind I have. But like the Wirths', on Slough Pond, and the Perrys', on Lieutenant Island?" The idea had taken hold. "When do you want to start?" I asked. "Maybe you weren't listening to me, Mom. I'm taking a new job. I can't quit before I even show up for work." I could see she had misinterpreted me; I could also see that her response was perfectly reasonable. I'd put my foot in it again. Why does Beth bring out the worst in me?

As she was getting ready to leave, Beth asked, in the most casual, offhand manner, if her father and I were okay. "Why do you ask?" She shrugged and said, "Just a feeling. No big deal. It's not any of my business, really," she said. She frowned. "I forgot to tell you," she said. Andy had sent her an e-mail. He was working for an outfit that put on events for charities and other organizations that wanted to call attention to themselves. "Sounds like a perfect fit," I said.

I told Tom I was thinking of going to Truro the following weekend.

"Oh? Sorry I won't be able to come with you."

"That's okay," I said. "Do you mind if I ask why?"

"You know that committee I'm on, the one that interviews candidates for that rare open slot in the department? We agreed to meet this guy on Saturday morning. It was the only day the man could make it — he looks awfully good on paper."

I nodded. "You don't mind?"

"I do mind. I could use a day or two of R & R."

My response, drawn out of a habit of thirty years, was automatic. I went over to him and put a hand on his arm. Once, this juncture had produced sparks. I was surprised now that it produced nothing at all, as if his arm belonged to a corpse — or was it my hand that had no life left in it? I wanted so badly to feel something that, without meaning to, I half-choked on the word "Tom!" "What's the matter, Dannie?" he said. "Did I do something?" I told him of course not. Which one of the two takes the blame for letting the tape run out and failing to insert another?

The Truro house smelled lovely, like an ancient pine pillow along with something a little bit off, like the shells of tiny creatures. I opened a window and a cold bay breeze filled the rooms, freshening the air inside. I looked out the window, trying to get the two parts of myself to make up and form one whole. I was sure I could do this here and I did feel a little better. I phoned Raymie. Mitch answered. After identifying myself, I said I'd like to speak to Raymie. I could hear him call "honey" — that must be Raymie. "Hi, honey," I said. She asked what I was doing in Truro. Her voice sounded different — a little strained.

I asked her if she'd like to come to my house for lunch the next day. "Why don't you come over here?" she said. "I've got this huge refrigerator full of goodies. Mitch won't mind. He said he'd like to see you."

We went back and forth until finally I agreed.

The next morning I worked hard on a new project and actually produced one page out of five attempts that didn't make me want to throw up. Work does not grow easier. When I finally looked at the clock, I saw that it was time to quit.

Should I change my grungy Truro clothes, the old jeans and the stained sweatshirt threadbare at the neck? I decided I would, then changed my mind. I said goodbye to Marshall (assuring him I'd take him for a walk later), left the house and walked down the beach and then up the stairs to the Brenner house. I took a deep breath: "Hello?"

Raymie opened the sliding door and came out to meet me. She hugged me. "I'm so glad to see you, Dannie. God, I've missed you. Come on in." I smelled musky perfume on her neck. As soon as she stepped back, I realized that she had transformed herself into a Ralph Lauren girl — crisp, clean, yet outdoorsy in perfectly creased and spotless designer chinos, a heavy coral pink turtleneck sweater with flecks of silver in it and a pair of unscuffed Docksiders over crew socks. On her wrist was a gold chain bracelet with a charm hanging off it that probably read TO HIS HONEY FROM HER MITCH. Her hair was brushed straight and looked to me as if it had spent some time in a beauty parlor, getting spitted and polished. Clothes remake the woman.

I nearly said, "Raymie, is that you?" I suppose she could have gone another way: jeans that hugged her butt, high heels, a tight shirt (wasn't that how she had described Ruthie at the P'Town restaurant?). But Mitch had halfway figured out that Truro was not Miami and had opted for L.L.Bean, Eddie Bauer and the more or less WASPy style. Halfway because, as I noted earlier, every item of clothing was spanking new or clean or free of anything that makes a thing look worn. The classiest gent I know in Truro — someone with a true Cape Cod heart in his chest and a laid-back style that has nothing to do with the hard work it takes to write plays — seems, to a stranger, like a man who spends his mornings rummaging through Dumpsters.

"Mitch is on the phone — as usual," she said. "Can I get you something to drink?"

I could hear Mitch talking in a room off the living room, which had been supplied with furniture not really hideous but far too large. The leather couch, for instance, could have held six adults side by side, the armchair facing it, two. Substantial, they were built to last a thousand years. Raymie invited me to come into the kitchen while she finished working on our meal. "Mitch wanted us to have lobsters," she said. "So that's what we're having."

It was one of those times when things are over the top but you're glad anyway. Mitch's voice grew louder, although I still couldn't hear what he was saying. A minute later, he appeared in the kitchen, a white sweater draped across his shoulders, its sleeves tied together over his breastbone. His eyebrows seemed bushier than ever. Leaning on an ebony cane with a silver handle, he said hello to me. I thought I saw a smirk flash quickly across his features. I stuck out my hand, which he shook.

"Got everything straightened out?" Raymie asked.

"Sonofabitch is still holding out on me," he said. Then, to me. "We don't want to talk business here, do we? How are those beasties coming along, honey?"

"Another few minutes, Mitch," Raymie said. I tried to read the extent of her affection for him but was unable to pierce her chirpiness. I've probably spent far too much time trying to decide whether or not human leopards can change their spots. Some people seem to be able to do it. These are the folks who start out as scamps and end up as pious purveyors of virtue, like Charles Colson, the man who lied for Richard Nixon, preaching the Gospel from jail. And other species, like the man who started out a rabbi and ended up as a NASCAR driver. Are these genuine changes, or are they simply the flip side of an overfocused personality? While I dealt with my lobster — they had the right little forks and picks to pry out the claw meat — I tried to get a read on Raymie and found her nothing but insistently and charmingly attentive to Mitchell Brenner. She did all the serving and clearing — just as she had in her B&B. Except now it was accompanied by the sort of affectionate gesture or tone of voice you save for someone near and dear to you. I couldn't imagine that she was in love with him, failing, perhaps, to empathize and only judging from my own heart. I could no more love this man than I could Dick Cheney, our vice president, a man with money motives so obvious they stuck out like the needles on the back of a porcupine. What was change anyway? Had B been lurking inside A all those years and finally got out? Or had B killed A and snatched his body? I looked at Raymie, listened to her speak, watched as she ever so lightly brushed Mitch's cheek with her hand, and I could not, for the life of me, understand what she was really up to.

The meal was pleasant enough. Mitch didn't do anything obnoxious. It was just his attitude — arrogant, dismissive, humorless — that bothered me, along with his tying almost any subject one of us brought up to money. Real estate, of course, but *swimming?* At one point, as Raymie and I were comparing bodies of water in which to swim — bay, ocean, pond — he educated us on the economics of what he called the "swimsuit industry" and how it relies chiefly on winter sales because rich women go south when it's cold and don't mind paying a hundred bucks or more for a tiny piece of spandex or whatever it was swimsuits were made out of, and on and on, Raymie composing her features into tolerant enjoyment: "Doesn't the dear man know a lot about a lot of things?" I couldn't wait to get away, my distress fed both by Raymie's new persona and Mitch's sensibility.

And then he surprised me once again, by looking out over the bay and sighing with obvious pleasure. And it wasn't just the lobsters, and the raspberries Raymie served for dessert, it was the waterscape below and stretching to the horizon. It was a calm day and the seabirds rose and fell, afloat on light currents of air. How could a man like Mitch like what I like? It almost made me angry.

"I ought to be getting back," I said.

"Oh, stay for a while," Raymie said. I noticed that Mitch didn't echo the invitation. "Well, maybe I'll stay a few minutes."

"You gals do your thing," Mitch said, "I've got a couple of calls to make." He disappeared into the room where he'd been on the phone earlier, leaving Raymie and me with a shitload of things unsaid. But how can you ask your bosom friend what she's doing with a man like Mitch? As for Raymie, she no doubt felt my disapproval, the way you always know when someone close to you hates what you're doing but refuses to say so.

"Come and see my garden," she said.

"It's out in back." We slipped out through a slider to the land side of the house. It wasn't warm enough for any flowers, so, except for evergreens and heather, you could only see the beds she had dug. Raymie told me which flowers were going to come up where. Off to one side was a plot where, she said, she was going to plant vegetables: squash, eggplant, tomatoes, spinach. "We brought in two tons of top-soil," she said. "It's so nice not having to worry about where every penny for anything you want is going to come from."

"Anything new on Halliday?" I asked.

"Apparently, they're still on his trail. At least they claim they are. How is one to know? How can someone like that disappear? You know what I think? All this stuff about terrorists in our midst? People like Halliday are small potatoes compared to some guy planning to blow up the Brooklyn Bridge. They're just too busy looking for diaperheads to bother with the likes of our whack job."

"Sounds right," I said. I was so close to telling her about David Lipsett that I could feel the words crowding my mouth, pushing against my lips. In the old days, before Mitch screwed around with her head, she would have got an earful: "I met this man and it's driving me crazy. I can't stop thinking about him. He seems to like me, but I'm not sure whether with him it's just sex or something else as well. He's in New York, which of course makes it easier for me on the one hand and harder on the other. Easier because I can't flop into his lap whenever I feel like it, but harder because I can't see him and his adorable face. What do you think I ought to do?"

And the old Raymie would answer, "And what about Tom? Are you ready to dump your husband of thirty years for a man you hardly know?"

Mitch appeared at that moment, holding a sheet of paper. "Raymie," he said, "that son of a bitch Halliday, or whatever his name is, just sent me this." He thrust the sheet of paper at Raymie, who took it, squinted at it and told Mitch that she'd left her reading glasses inside. "Here, I'll read it to you," Mitch said, grabbing back the piece of paper. "It says here on this e-mail, 'I'll be back to finish the job.' It's signed 'cleanser666.' " He stopped there, letting it sink in. "That should be easy enough to trace," I said. Mitch looked at me as if he had just found out I was retarded. "No, Dannie," he said. "You can use any number of sender names. Then you just go

to the local library, sit down at the terminal and grind out your message."
Raymie said, "This really sucks. How does
he get away with it?"

"Who's to stop him?" Mitch said.

"I'm going to call Pete Savage," Raymie
said.

"What's a Provincetown cop going to do
for you that Jerry Braccio can't?" I assumed
that Mr. Braccio was the P.I. Mitch had
hired. It seemed to me that neither he nor
Savage had done that much to find the
man, but nobody asked me for my opinion
so I kept my mouth shut.

Raymie went into the house to phone
Savage. Mitch looked at the e-mail once
again, then folded it neatly and stuck it in
the back pocket of his shorts. "It takes all
kinds," he said, more to himself than to
me. I thought this was a healthy reaction,
considering, and I told him so. "What are
you going to do?" he said. "Build a bunker
and spend the rest of your life in there?
Hire armed guards? That's not my idea of
a life."

I have to admit, I admired him for this
little declaration. I asked him to say
goodbye to Raymie for me and thanked
him again for lunch.

"No problem," he said.

149

I walked double-time back to my house, hoping to work off some of the large meal. I was thinking about Raymie and realizing, with a pang, that she had gone over to the other side, the side that has their garbage collected rather than hauling it to the dump, the side that has all their forks and knives from the same set, the side that never eats at Moby Dick's on Route 6. For my money, Moby's serves up the best fish on the Outer Cape, but if you don't get there for lunch at eleven forty-five, you better be prepared to cool your heels for at least fifteen minutes. It was not so much about how much money you had as about how what you did with it looked to other people. Raymie and Mitch were together now, joined in a way that erased what had been basic differences. So that, really, they were more like one than two. Could I put up with it?

I was watching the news at six when I learned that someone had splashed blood — they hadn't determined what kind of blood, human or otherwise — against the front door of a house in Grosse Pointe, Michigan, a fancy suburb of Detroit, and also left an anti-Semitic message. The sheriff of Wayne County came on, standing in front of what was clearly a McMonster, pillared, gabled, towered, with twin urns crowded with what looked like fake flowers, one on each side of the front door, and a curved window two stories high smack in the middle. The sheriff shifted uncomfortably in the eye of the camera, his glasses catching light and sending it back at us. "This is a first for us here in this community," he said. "We're not ruling out calling it a hate crime." We were invited to tune in to a late-night investigative report focusing on ecoterrorism and anti-Semitism. It sounded as if they couldn't make up their minds whether it had to do with the size of the house or the ethnicity of its owners. Had Halliday fired another round in his campaign to save the world from Jewish excess?

I called Raymie and told her to turn on the news. "I've seen it," she said. "Maybe he runs a training camp for Jew-hating ecoterrorists who need to demonstrate their distaste for the way other people live. Why don't they get a life?"

I told Raymie I wouldn't be surprised if the trasher turned out to be Halliday. "He seems to like big houses."

I was mildly joking about something that wasn't the least bit funny. How could you

lead a normal life when maniacs lurked behind every dune and hedge, waiting to get
you? The answer was, you couldn't. How
did the people living in Israel get used to
it? Go to the beauty parlor to have your
hair done and when you return, you find
your apartment building has turned into a
pile of rubble.

Raymie said Mitch thought it was
Halliday. He'd been on the phone again
with his private investigator. "Really," she
said, "I wish he'd stop spending so much
money on this manhunt."

Could I ask her just how much was so
much? Did I care?

I continued to hear from David Lipsett,
mainly via e-mail, one of the most useful
inventions, right up there after the paper
napkin. His messages were carefully
crafted and seemed to be bristling with
subtext. "I'm sitting at my desk thinking
about how best to use your work; you have
many talents." "When you come to New
York again, I think it's important that we
talk about your future."

Meanwhile, Tom and I had drifted into
what surely was the last phase before a
couple split: no yelling, recriminations, sly
tricks, competitive games. I suppose it was

something like what often comes over a person about to commit suicide — the rough places go absolutely flat. If you're just about to ingest a handful of pills, does it matter that you owe the MasterCard people fifteen thousand bucks, or that your brother has just been convicted of aggravated assault, or that your spouse called you a rotten pig? We had retreated into a freezer, surrounded not by haunches of uncooked prime beef and legs of lamb but by memories — and both of us too cold to talk. How had we ended up here? From desire and affection to indifference and irritation — I grew to hating the way he chewed on his eyeglasses, a habit I had once found sweet and boyish. I couldn't stand the way he picked at his fingernails, sometimes until they bled.

David occupied more and more of the space inside my head. I sent him an e-mail telling him I was thinking of coming to New York in the next few weeks — would he have time to look at some more of my photographs? He answered back within an hour. "A terrific idea! When?" I looked through my portfolios and decided that only one of them would do. So I took my camera and prowled my Watertown neighborhood, caught some pleasing moments

— a fat old man eating an ice-cream cone with the melted stuff dripping across his fist, two people leaning against a car, talking fervently. I found a homeless woman huddled under a filthy blanket in the unused doorway of a hardware store. I took her picture without her knowing it — this is something I don't like to do, but I did it anyway because she had, under the grime, a beautiful face.

I had the pictures developed and printed, chose a few and stuck them between the jaws of my portfolio, and picked out the clothes I would wear while in New York. I knew the photographs were just an excuse to bring David and me together, a nice, businesslike convenience, the subtext of our meeting. The pictures carried the weight of what did not have to be said.

I told Tom I was going to New York. I expected him to say "Again? What for?" But he didn't. He said, "That's nice."

"Tom," I said. "When I get back, don't you think you and I should talk about things?"

"What things?"

"Us."

"What about us?"

"Something's happened to what we used to be."

"We got old," he said.

I told him to speak for himself. "And anyway, what does how old we are have to do with anything?" I was being as disingenuous as anyone trying to score emotional points. Of course age had something to do with it. I wish I could have accused him of beastly behavior, but I couldn't. He was good old Tom who had lapsed into a routine that no longer included me. His work absorbed him like a bride. And maybe he was, as they say, "seeing" someone else as well. But that wasn't it either.

"For chrissake, Tom, can't you even look at me?"

"Why are you yelling, Dannie?"

"Because it's so much louder than gnashing my teeth."

I guess we had stepped out of the freezer for a moment and although we warmed up a little, it was not a success.

This trip to New York, I stayed at a hotel that I found on the Internet by telling hotels.com that I didn't want to spend more than a hundred and twenty-five dollars. It was a perfectly nice place in Midtown, although the lobby looked as if nothing had been seriously done to it for twenty-five years or so. I brought my portfolio over to David's office, as I had the last time. He looked at the photos and pronounced them "interesting." Then he reminded me that he was a children's book editor. I asked him why not find someone to write a children's book about a beautiful homeless woman. "Who is really a breathtaking princess transformed by an evil witch jealous of her beauty?" asked David.

"I'm crazy about it," I said.

"God, you look good," he said.

I thanked him, eyes lowered.

"I have a meeting uptown this afternoon," he said. "How about dinner?"

"I don't see why not," I said. Actually, I saw one big reason why not and I was fooling myself if I believed he didn't too. It was how we all seem to know the rules even if we haven't played this particular game before. Except in movies, and HBO, the true, lusty message hides under layers of rectitude, politesse, innuendo.

"Good," David said. "I was hoping you'd say that. Look, I know what you're probably thinking. You're a married woman, I'm single. I assume we both saw the movie *Fatal Attraction.*" (I nodded.) "That movie either did a great deal of harm or an awful lot of good — I can't decide which — but what happens is everyone is scared to indulge in a friendship. You and I have been working together for years, for chrissake, what's the big deal?"

"Did I say anything?"

"I guess not," he said. "I sound defensive?"

I nodded again.

"Well," he said, standing and looking at his watch. "I'll pick you up at your hotel, say seven-thirty?"

I spent the afternoon in Soho, going to half a dozen galleries where I saw work that my art teacher in college would have dismissed as "junk," not willing to give it half a chance. Aesthetics had given way to emotion — "How romantic," I thought, "just like the nineteenth century." In one gallery I saw four pairs of soccer balls hanging from the ceiling in soft net bags, suggesting, if anything, testicularity. Was it art? It made you wonder what, in fact, art was. And all the time I was in and out of these places, along with other visitors, most of them in the most amazing outfits and colored hair and rings in their noses, ears, eyelids, lips, tongue (only one of those) and I could only imagine where else, having heard that some men had pierced their penises — a practice that apparently met with the approval of the women they penetrated. Ouch!

Art had turned a corner while I was doing my little thing with my children's books. Beautiful had been relegated to the hinged box in the attic and you didn't want to go up there because the dust was so thick. And there were mice. I suppose that was okay, mainly because it meant that people who did art moved on from one thing to the next. If they hadn't, we would still paint pictures like Giotto. Still, it felt odd to gasp rather than sigh when looking at some object — let's say a toilet with a cracked seat — set up in a gallery, starkly spotlit, when, if you saw the same thing in a bathroom your only reaction would be to be careful sitting down. Are there little old ladies still painting watercolors of the fruit trees beyond the porch? It's nice to think so, except their work won't hang in Soho, New York. I don't suppose they give a hoot. And if they do give a hoot, a small one, they do so while consigning the newest "art" to the degenerate pile. Was it ever any different?

While I was educating myself in the new edgy aesthetic, I was thinking of David Lipsett with guilt and a longing of the sort usually embraced by girls just into puberty. Did I consider myself to have stepped over some line not endorsed by conventional society? Not at all. As a matter of fact, I was sure I was joining those women — and, according to *Newsweek*, there were an awful lot of them — who felt that if they had to have sex with the same man for the rest of their lives they'd kill themselves.

Briefly, I had considered going to see Ground Zero, getting a ticket and standing in line, maybe for several hours, along with hundreds of others whose motives for looking down into the enormous gash in the ground were murky at best. It wasn't clear to me at all what makes people visit places, once perfectly ordinary, but now covered with the patina of the sacred. I've done it myself. The year I graduated from college, I went to Aix, where Cézanne lived for a while, looking at his house and trying to take in something from it, as if he were still hanging about the place, giving lessons to gifted students. But I hesitated about Ground Zero. There was something ghoulish about; it would be like viewing an operation on your own abdomen after being shot. My imagination — along with the television and the *New York Times* — had provided me with enough visual stuff to fill my mind for the rest of my life. So I didn't go.

Besides, I was nervous and impatient. I went back to my hotel, slipped the card into the slot — who would have thought, fifty years earlier, that a plastic rectangle would replace a brass key? — undressed and took a shower. The cake of soap smelled like generic flower, the shampoo came in a bottle the size of a container of baby aspirin. But the towel was nice and big and soft. I wrapped it around me, pulled back the cover on the double bed and lay there for a while, watching the news. I like to watch the New York City news when I'm there, things you're not apt to see elsewhere: a delicatessen in Queens robbed by two little girls with fake handguns; the kid who dropped his girlfriend's baby out of a fourth-story window; the mayor cutting a ribbon with a theatrical pair of shears at the opening of a Wal-Mart in the South Bronx; Bill Clinton, caressed by a crowd in Harlem. Everything very specific, and the cameras right there, just minutes after the crime or on the spot with Clinton and the mayor. There's a sort of small-town intimacy to these TV images, the guys in the studio doing a minimum of chitchat. There was no minibar in the room — what did I expect for under a hundred and thirty-five bucks? — or I would have treated myself to a ten-dollar, eight-ounce bottle of wine, to take the edge off. David said he would pick me up. When the phone rang, I was dressed and putting on my

160

makeup with shaking fingers. I told him I'd be down in five minutes. I was ready in three but held back for another two.

When the elevator door opened, he was waiting right there; I nearly bumped into him. "You look great," he said. He seemed to say that a lot. Did he really mean it, or was he nervous like I was?

"We're going to Benno's, a sort of bistro. Is that all right with you?"

"Sounds fine," I said. He could have said Burger King and that would have been all right too. At that moment, putting a hand on my right ear, I realized I had forgotten to put on my earrings.

"Is something the matter?" he said.

"I forgot my earrings."

"You don't need them."

"I do."

"Do you want to go back for them?" he said.

"I guess not."

"You have lovely ears." He wasn't looking at me when he said this. The force of his feeling for me was like the flash of heat when you open the oven door to see how the roast is doing.

He was wearing a gray shirt with a banded collar, buttoned up to the last button, khaki chinos and a black jacket that could have been cashmere, something very soft-looking anyway. To me he looked New York cool.

"Would you mind walking?" David asked. "It's about eight blocks."

I told him I loved walking in the City.

Throughout most of the meal — and it was very good, portions just the right size, exotic marinated fish — we talked about work, mine and his. He enjoyed his job, that was obvious. I asked him if he had ever tried to write a book himself and he said, "When I retire. I've got a couple of ideas I'd like to try out."

I could hardly swallow the incredible food in front of me. All I could focus on was, when were we going to jump into bed together? His tongue darted around when he took a bite off his fork, like a lizard. I wanted him to kiss me. I wanted him to kiss me every little where.

He hadn't told me what he did for sex. Did I really want to know? Did he do it with Ashley? When I was very young, my mother assured me that all men slept with their secretaries and I believed it for the longest time. No secretaries today. Today they were "assistants"; everyone wanted an upgrade. Ashley had no meat on her bones, skinny little thing. Her bones stuck out like a pre-corpse's. But even that wouldn't keep her boss from doing it with her, though he might have liked something more to grab onto. I wondered if David was browsing in the same general area that I was. Then I realized I must have been nuts. Why me when there were so many delicious younger, juicier morsels within arm's reach. Why me? What did he want with a woman deep into middle age with tired lines around her mouth, a vertical crease on her brow and about fifteen more pounds than she needed. I didn't get it; it was a near-impossible leap for me to believe that if, in fact, sex was his plan, I was the target.

"Would you like some dessert? The biscotti's great. Or espresso?" David asked me.

"I couldn't eat another thing," I said. "And coffee keeps me awake. No. I'm all set, thanks."

David got the bill and paid with an American Express card. I wanted to ask him if he was putting this dinner on his expense account, but didn't have the nerve.

"Well," he said as we left Benno's and stood outside on the sidewalk, "where would you like to go now?"

"We probably ought to go to my place. It's closer," I said.

CHAPTER 7

As David closed the door of room number 1208, I began to imagine us as two characters in a movie, and this put me at an awkward distance from the scene, as if I were sitting in the audience, making judgments: Were the characters "realistic"? Did the plot follow some basic understanding of cause and effect? How about "motivation" — did we have a clue as to why they were doing what they were doing? Then I leapt back into the action, where the clichés made me extremely self-conscious. The camera had focused on me, and beyond that sat an unseen director watching my every move and telling me what to do. Was this going to be a teen flick, where you rip off your clothes willy-nilly, tearing buttons from their anchors, leaving your things in a heap on the carpet, flinging yourselves onto the bed and going at it like two beasts? Or would it be an "autumn of life" story, with nostalgic background music, up, while you do a languorous mating dance, with whiskey sipped to help you bury the shyness and trepidation?

"Nice room," David said.

"It's okay."

"I don't suppose you have anything to drink?"

"As a matter of fact, I don't."

"No minibar?"

I shook my head. We were standing motionless, waiting to be cued, the hesitancy factor about equal in each of us. "Well." Hesitancy was now joined by reluctance. "Do you get high?" he said, reaching into his coat pocket.

"Once in a while," I said. "But right now it seems too much like *Annie Hall*. I think I'll give it a pass."

What was I doing here? The wild and windy attraction had lost some of its power, downsizing from an outright hurricane to a tropical depression.

"Why don't I order something from room service?" David said.

"There's a package store just down the street," I said.

"What's a package store?"

"A liquor store," I said.

"Hmmm." Was he reminded, as I was, that two hundred and fifty miles lay between us, as authentic an obstacle as a tree, fallen across the road?

"Do we really need it?"

"I guess not," David said. He looked as if he felt exactly as I did. The oddest element of my hesitation had, I think, to do with the way I looked undressed. While David had the slimness of a person who never had to worry about calories, I was a "before" picture, familiar to readers of diet pill ads, lumpy around the thighs, heavy-breasted, my abdomen, once flat, now rounded like the second trimester of pregnancy.

"I feel silly," I said.

"Don't," David said. "You're anything but."

"Do we really want to do this?"

"I do. I was hoping — given plenty of evidence, as a matter of fact — that you did too . . ." He trailed off. Next, he would be accusing me of being a tease, the ultimate male put-down. I suppose you can't blame them — their dicks are all dressed for the party and they have nowhere to go.

We sparred for a few minutes more, and then, like some old married couple, we offered to let the other use the bathroom, then quietly took off our clothes and, me first, got into bed. The sheets were smooth and cold, like water when you first lower yourself into the pond. David talked to me softly, close to my ear. He told me I was a lovely person inside a lovely body.

I protested that I was too fat and he said most women in New York were too thin. That's all they thought about, staying a size eight. "Eight?" I said. "It's more like a four." I told him I knew someone who was a size zero. All the while his hands were skimming my body, landing one place, then another. He brushed me lightly with his penis, back and forth, barely touching me, and taking me to a pitch of excitement so taut I made a kind of screeching sound, as if I were being strangled; it was a noise like none I'd ever made before. "You like that?" he said. "Oh my God, yes," I said, no longer looking on self-consciously, but right in the thick of things. He entered me easily, smoothly, then quickly pulled out. He did this several times, with no apparent effort, and each time, I rose up on my hips to meet him, then fell back as he withdrew. This was exquisitely inflammatory. "My God," I said. "What are you doing?" "Getting you ready," he said. "You weren't ready before."

"I am now," I whispered. He lay square on top of me, supporting himself on his elbows and leaving me plenty of room to thrash around in and to let my body answer whatever question his body asked me. Then, at his urging, we reversed roles, with me astride his hips, with my poor old breasts hanging down. I looked at his face; he was grinning, his eyes squeezed shut. "You're amazing," he said. His arms and legs were thinner than Tom's, his torso longer, his chest hairier; it was covered with hair, curly black, thick as weeds. His penis was smaller than Tom's, not much but still enough for me to be aware of the differences. Nevertheless, we fit as if we had been custom-ordered for each other. We fell briefly asleep, then, waking, made love again. "You're crying," David said.

"I'm not."

"What's this, then?" He had lifted a tear off my face; it glistened on his finger like a tiny pearl.

"Because to be this happy is to know what you don't have most of the time — and that's terribly sad."

He made it clear that this could go on for a long time. It was up to me. Then he told me that I was astonishing, adorable — there was that word again. I suggested that he just might be especially horny. "No," he said. "It's you."

I accused him of flattery and he said he didn't want to ever hear me talk that way again. He was so serious. He said I should be able to accept a compliment without turning it on its head. "I suppose you're right," I said. "But I really don't know what to do with praise from the outside."

Then, out of the blue he asked me if I knew that he was Jewish.

"Well, I guess I just assumed it," I told him. "Why, does it bother you?"

"No, not really. I guess I'm just a little sensitive."

"Nobody gives a hoot anymore — except maybe my mother." He asked about my mother and I gave him a thumbnail sketch, bathing the picture in a faintly rosy light.

"Okay," he said when I was finished. "And my mother would call you a shiksa."

"So we're even?"

"We're even." He smothered me with passionate kisses.

I didn't give a hoot whether or not David was Jewish. I had, years before, assumed he was, because his name said he was. But it hadn't even occurred to me to view his Jewishness as of any more consequence than his shirt size. My mother, on the other hand, would have said something like "Oh, *really?*" had I been foolish enough to tell her I had a Jewish lover. She was born in the so-called Roaring Twenties — although it's not clear who was doing the roaring. People like my mother didn't know any Jews back then, except maybe the man who owned the local pharmacy. Did I care that David was not a Christian? Not a bit. And then I realized that maybe it did add a little something exotic to the mix, a spice I found tasty, like fenugreek. So, basically, his Jewishness was a plus, not a minus.

"Why is it so important to you? It's not to me."

"We're sensitive — no, 'oversensitive' says it better. It's like an atavistic shudder. But you haven't answered my question," David said. He was staring at the ceiling.

I told him I'd answer if he didn't let it become a thing between us and that I didn't know what was going to happen or if these few hours would ever be repeated. He interrupted me with assurances that they would be repeated. I told him I couldn't go on cheating on Tom. "And you're not even Jewish," he said. "It's not how I want to live," I said. "Besides, everyone I know who's had an affair says it wrecks your work, all that sneaking around and telling lies — it takes too much time and energy." I turned on my side and lightly touched the hair on his chest — what a novelty! "You're my first," I said.

"Okay," he said. I thought for a moment

that he was going to ask me how he compared, but thank God he spared me that. Men are so hung up on their dicks — but I knew that already.

I told him it was my turn to ask him a personal question.

"I guess it is," he said. "What would you like to know?"

"How did you lose your little finger?"

"Oh this?" he said, holding up his hand and looking at it as if seeing it for the first time. "Fireworks, when I was a kid," he said. "I got too close, the thing went off before we were ready. I was with my brother, Freddie. He got his eyebrows singed off. They never grew back."

It was a pretty good story, although not quite on a dramatic par with alligator or thresher or chain saw.

"You don't really need your little finger," he said. "I've stopped noticing."

I asked him how old he was when it happened. "Nine," he said, "and fearless."

David spent the night with me in the Rhinelander Hotel. The next morning, after making love a third time, we took a shower together, soaping each other's best parts, then dressed and went out for some breakfast. We found a deli cafeteria a few doors down the street, the sort of place that doesn't exist in Watertown or Truro, where you fill your plate with chunks of melon, berries, salmon and cream cheese and whatever else looks good from bowls sitting on ice on a steel buffet counter, and bring it to the cashier who weighs it and charges you accordingly. A swift river of people on their way to work came in to buy breakfast to go, coffee in paper mugs, bagels slathered with cream cheese, a cup of fresh cut-up fruit. "Are you sad?" I asked David. The sex magnetism was still severe; it was all I could do to keep from leaning over and kissing him on the mouth.

"I'm sad. Because you're leaving."

"I'm too old," I said, leaving most of what I was thinking unsaid: We're not kids. I have a husband and a life I've constructed out of a medium-sized talent and true grit. What I feel might be love. On the other hand, it's just as likely to be a sudden rush of passion, mixed with a sense of going nowhere and desperate to move — anywhere. The bottom line was, whenever sex is involved, you don't know what you feel — except that you want more sex. You have to engage in the daily comings and goings for months, maybe years, before you know whether it's love or just sex that's gluing the two of you together. Do you really like the guy? Do you both think the same people are weird? Do you both dismiss New Agey thinking as stupid? Can you stand his nasty habits? Does he genuinely care about what happens to you?

"Too old for what? Not too old to make me your slave."

"You're kidding, yes? I don't want you to be my slave."

"I *am* kidding," he said. "But I mean, after last night, we've got to be more than working friends. I see us together. Or rather, I want us to be together. You have a lot of thinking to do, I know that. It's easier for me."

Neither of us had said *I love you,* among the most delicate phrases in the English language — unless you're a sociopath who wouldn't hesitate to use it to secure any number of things you fancy. For most of us, it's a sacred phrase, to be employed only when the mixture contains exactly the right amounts of its assorted elements: sex, pleasure, warmth, reciprocity, humor and, above all else, the appetite — and stamina — to spend years together without descending into boredom, resentment, betrayal, ill will. I tried to imagine eating breakfast with David Lipsett for the next twenty-plus years of eight o'clocks. It was pretty hard, mainly because he was — I faced it — a stranger. That I felt, at that moment, drinking the remarkably good coffee he had bought me, that we were somehow suited to each other in ways that even Tom and I, at the beginning, had not been, that our sensibilities dovetailed, was only an index of how I felt at that moment. How would I feel next week, in six months, in three years?

"You're certainly not making it any easier for me," I said.

David looked at his watch. "It's after nine-thirty," he said. "I've got to get to work. What are you going to do?"

"I was thinking I should be getting back to Watertown."

"I'm going to miss you."

"I'm going to miss you too."

We left the question of "us" hanging. When I got back to Watertown, my mind started working properly again; its parts having been silently realigned. I hardly knew David. What was I thinking? Half my life had been spent with Tom, and I could let it go more easily than I could a lost wallet?

For the next week or so, Tom seemed to be a shadow in the house, arranging his schedule so that he only came home late at night and left, most days, before I was fully awake. Where he worked, rocket scientists were a dime a dozen. Although there were none in the house on Whitman Street, there was no need: I would have had to be comatose not to realize that *he was trying to avoid me.* Nevertheless his shirts and underwear appeared daily in the bathroom hamper, waiting for me to put them in the washing machine and return them, clean and folded, to their owner. This was my marriage.

I retreated to Truro. When I arrived, the wind was ferocious — loud as a train, bending tree branches and whipping sand against the windows. Raymie and Mitch were in Florida, in a condo owned by Mitch, escaping the coldest, dampest, windiest weeks of the Truro winter. I was feeling so low that I turned on the television. There's little or no cable on the Outer Cape, although some folks have satellite dishes that skew around crazily in the wind. I watched the news, stunned by the consistency of George Bush's instincts, which struck me as instinctively wrong-headed, mean-spirited, and sometimes tyrannical. He seemed to be convinced that business was more important than people and that this should come as a surprise was in itself a surprise; this depressed me and for the first time in years, the weather and isolation made me feel edgy in my house rather than snug. Just as I had made up my mind to go back to town right after breakfast the next day, the phone rang.

"Hi there, sweetheart, it's me, your New York admirer."

"David! How did you know I was here?"

"I called you in Watertown and a man, I guess it was your husband, said, 'She's not here.' I told him I was the editor of the book you were working on and that I needed to get in touch with you. He suggested e-mail. I don't think he was going to tell me where you were until I used the word 'urgent.' "

"So like Tom," I said. "Where are you?"

"You're not going to believe this," David said. "I'm at the Provincetown airport," he said. "I just used the bathroom and bought a Mars Bar from the vending machine."

"You're not serious." He assured me he was. "I'll come pick you up," I said. "But you know, you can't stay here."

"Oh?"

"This place has eyes and ears you wouldn't believe," I said. "They can see and hear through walls. And they get high on chewing over juicy bits of gossip: 'Who was that guy who got into Dannie Faber's car with her at the airport?' Bad enough I should be seen picking you up at the airport. I tell you what, I'll wait outside in the car. It'll take me about twenty minutes to get there. Is that okay?"

"Are you sure you're not being just a wee bit paranoid?"

"I'm sure. David?"

"Yes?"

"Damn — I can't wait to see you."

David was standing outside the front door of our spiffy new airport, since 2001 fitted out with the latest in security equipment, including a giant machine that X-rays every bit of your luggage, including carry-ons and laptops, and makes you step on a scale right in front of everyone. The smile he produced when he saw me melted the hesitation that had been forming like a chunk of ice over my heart on the drive over. He tossed his shoulder bag into the back seat, got into the car and leaned over to kiss me on the cheek. "You smell good," he said.

"You sure no one saw you?" I said.

"A couple of people saw me," he said. "I'm not exactly invisible. But they didn't know where I was headed. Although, come to think of it, a guy in coveralls gave me a fishy look . . .”

“You’re kidding, aren’t you?”

“Yes, I’m kidding.”

“It’s not funny, David. I don’t feel right about this.”

“You’re ambivalent. That’s okay with me, honeypot. I wouldn’t like you so much if you didn’t feel conflicted. It’s going to come out fine, I know it, whatever happens. Right now, I want you to tell me what we’re seeing. Believe it or not, I’ve never been out this way before. I always meant to, but just never got around to it — ’til now.”

Just having him six inches away set me on fire. Maybe I was going through a second puberty, with all systems electrified, ready for someone to hit the button. I hadn’t felt so excited since the first year I was married to Tom. “You’re passing Pilgrim Lake,” I told him. I cut over to the shore drive to be off the highway and close to the bay. It was lead-gray, with whitecaps. “It’s kind of bleak,” David said.

“You should see it in early July. Pink and red galore, everything in bloom. It knocks your socks off.”

I told him this bleakness created the kind of tension that exists only in a place where the seasons are discrete and distinct in the extreme. "It's not like Antigua or the South Pole. What you see and feel in winter isn't anything like what you see and feel in summer. It keeps you on your toes." He smiled at me indulgently and I realized I was sounding pedantic, but it seemed more important for me to underscore my devotion to my home than to achieve the right insouciant tone.

When we got to the house, I was really nervous about being seen with David. I looked in every direction, but of course, since I was out of sight of anyone on my stretch of the beach, I needn't have bothered. Still, my conscience was bothering me. David represented the New York part of me and when he came to the Cape, he had changed the rules, making them harder to obey.

"You first," he said as I gestured for him to go inside. So he followed me in. Once the front door was behind us, he put his hands on my shoulders and his eyes focused on mine, told me that he'd been terrified the plane would be grounded and he wouldn't be able to make it.

"What did you tell your boss?" I said.

"*I'm* my boss," he said. "I told me I was going to spend a night with the love of my life."

This did not seem to require any sort of response, so I asked him what he had told Ashley. "I said I'd be back day after tomorrow. She's got my cell phone number if there's an emergency." I wondered what sort of emergency might befall an editor of children's books; it wasn't exactly like working for the Defense Department.

"Where's the bedroom?" he said.

"I love your house," he said as he unbuckled his belt and stepped out of his chinos. His calves swelled with muscle. He pulled down his boxers. His penis pointed toward the ceiling. "Aren't you going to get undressed?" he said.

"Oh." I had been transfixed, watching him. "Look at it!"

He looked down. " 'She plays me like a lute, what tune she will, / No string in me but trembles at her touch.' But in your case, you don't even have to touch me."

"That's nice," I said. "Who wrote that? You?"

"I'm flattered. It's John Masefield."

The only poem I ever heard Tom quote was "Casey at the Bat."

"Come on, let me see you, feel you, astonish you."

Sometime later — it was heavy dusk and

the wind had dropped almost entirely — David asked me whether I'd like to go out for dinner and, although the idea had definite appeal, I was afraid that one of our hungry gossips would see us together at one of the few restaurants still open.

"We could sit at separate tables," he said. "Or how about takeout?"

I shook my head. "No takeout. No Chinese restaurant, except at the Wellfleet miniature golf place. We'll have to rough it." There was enough in the freezer and the cabinets to make a soup, a couple of broiled chicken thighs, courtesy of the defrost setting on the microwave oven, and a canned bean salad. David had brought a bottle of Pinot Grigio, which he uncorked. I lit two candles. "Voilà," I said. "What do you think of the instant feast?"

As we sat down to eat, it struck me with some force that David had gone on as Tom's understudy in my domestic drama. How was he doing? He was doing just fine, outdoing the star, who had gone lazy and forgetful. He praised the food and he reached for my hand, holding it lightly. "I can't just go home and that's that," he said.

"What did you have in mind?" I said.

"I want to be with you all the time. You

181

give me the feeling that the world isn't going to hell."

"Isn't that optimism by default?" I said.

"Whatever. But I'm terribly lonely when I'm not with you; I thought I liked living alone. I don't. There's no one to listen to my bitching about the job. Besides, I think about you instead of my work. It's getting so that someone noticed in a meeting last week. He said, 'Head in the clouds again?' "

"We're not sixteen."

"Don't you think I've been over this territory a million times?"

"Of course, but I want to know what exactly you have in mind."

"You said that already."

"But you didn't answer."

"I want you to come to New York. I want us to live together." He paused, meaning to make the pause create an impact. "Why don't you say something?"

"I haven't found the right words." I got up and started pacing around the room, then stopped by the window below which lay the bay, reflecting the moonlight in silver slashes. It got to me; every time I looked at it, the bay was saying something different. David talked behind me, still sitting at the table. I could imagine the slight frown that went with the pretty speech. He told me that it was hardly news that my marriage had languished to a point where it seemed unlikely to get up and dance again. "The guy doesn't make you happy," he said. "Anyone can see that." He told me it was hardly news that he and I were great together, great in bed and out of it. "I make you feel good. You make me feel good. Tell me, Dannie, what's to keep you where you are?"

"Momentum," I said. "The known."

"You're afraid."

"You're right," I said. "I'm terrified."

The next day, after David left, I drove back to Watertown. No traffic. My neighbor, Alicia Baer, knocked on the back door as I was washing up after breakfast. "Something tells me you need to vent," she said. "Do you have a cup of coffee for me?" I gave her the coffee and asked how she knew so much about me. "All this coming and going," she said. "And always alone. Unnatural."

"Well . . ." Not only had she been spying on me, but she showed signs of being a bit more confrontational than I was prepared for. I suppose she figured that taking care of Marshall gave her the right to speak her mind. Besides, there was something forceful about her that obliged me to talk. I trusted her not to spread my good tidings all over the neighborhood. So I briefly painted a picture of me bathed by indecision and panic. She asked me if I loved David (I didn't tell her his last name) and I admitted that I thought so but I couldn't be sure. "At the beginning, how do you know whether it's love or lust?" Alicia didn't try to give me an acceptable answer. "The trouble is," I said, "by the time you find out which it really is, it's probably too late. The bridges have been burned." She reminded me that I didn't have to marry David. I could simply move in with him. The children were grown and I couldn't use them as an excuse to stay put. So the only real impediment was Tom. Wasn't that true? Alicia asked if my HMO provided for therapy. I don't know why it hadn't occurred to me to talk to a person whose profession it was to help you climb out of some muck you're in up to your eyeballs.

It was easy enough to find out that my HMO gives you ten almost free hours if you can convince your "primary caregiver" that you need it. Not for a second did I believe I was going nuts, but I was sure I could persuade my thirty-something doctor that my anxiety was as stubborn as a case of psoriasis. As it turned out, I didn't even have to visit her. When I called her, she asked me, "How old are you now?" and when I said fifty-three, she seemed to think it was standard for a woman my age to need help. "Just wait, honey," I thought. She gave me a couple of names and then reminded me that the kind of therapy they offered was strictly short-term. That was fine with me, as I wasn't up to doing any serious archeology. I made an appointment with a man named Gerard Casell — emphasis on the second syllable, as he told me over the phone when I called him Castle. He turned out to be in his forties, wore chinos (this seems to be the uniform for guys who wish they could wear jeans to work) and a tan polo shirt. He plied his trade in an office smaller than Raymie's new clothes closet. There were photographs on the wall — technicolor mountain scenes *avec* mist, which I assumed he had taken himself. We got down to business soon after "Tell me a little bit about yourself," when he asked, "And what brings you here?" I couldn't stop thinking of that scene in the movie *You Can Count on Me,* when the Laura Linney character goes to see her minister to confess to sleeping with her married boss and the minister refuses to tell her what she wants to hear, namely, "You're a sinner and you'll burn in hell if you don't stop right now — and maybe it's already too late."

"I'm cheating on my husband," I said. "If I were younger or a different sort of person, I assure you I wouldn't be here at all."

"What sort of person would that be?"

"A person who thinks it's okay so long as the husband doesn't find out. I guess I've got a fairly active conscience."

"I see," he said.

"So what do I do?"

Dr. Casell cleared his throat. "As I see it, you have two choices. Either you stop seeing this man or you develop a more passive conscience."

"How does one do that? I mean the conscience thing?"

"I suppose you consider the short-term and long-term risks and decide with your head, not the other place. How much does your commitment to your husband mean to you as against your devotion to — what did you say his name was?"

"David."

"David."

186

"Is it true," I asked, "that I'm somewhat old-fashioned? The younger generation is much cooler about sleeping around?"

"In my experience," Dr. Casell said, "they think they're cool, but no one wants his wife messing around with other men. It doesn't sit well."

"But it's perfectly fine the other way around? I mean, men don't think their wives will mind if they mess around — or maybe they don't think about their wives at all?"

"It's true," he said, "that men outnumber women in that category." He sighed deeply as if considering his own record.

Dr. Casell's phone rang, a red light on its dashboard blinking on and off like an impatient eye. He ignored it. But I couldn't. "You're not going to answer it?"

He said they would leave a message, having understood he was seeing a client. But it just kept ringing. Finally, neither of us willing to talk over it, he picked up. "Jerry Casell," he said. "When?" I looked down at my hands. The nails were permanently yellowish because of the paint. I wonder if he had noticed and figured me for a dirty person. "I'll take care of it ASAP," he said, frowning. Then he looked at me as if to say, "If you think I'm going to tell you what that was about, please disabuse yourself."

"We don't have much time left," he said. "My suggestion is, when you get home, make two lists on the same page. On one list I want you to write down all the reasons to stay with your husband that you can think of, including the little things, things you might think of as trivial, like what you do together on your birthday. Then, on the other list, all the reasons you can think of to leave him and be with David. Did I get the name right?"

I nodded. This man was asking me to reduce my earth-shaking, life-altering problem to two columns on a piece of paper. I couldn't believe he was serious. My face must have registered my skepticism, because he asked me whether I thought this "aid" was too mechanical. I nodded again. "Well, yes."

He told me it was just one of a number of ways of trying to solve a seemingly unsolvable life problem. "Why don't you just give it a try? It can't hurt. Do it right away, as soon as you get home. Make sure you write everything down and bring it with you when you come back." He looked straight at his clock. "I'm afraid that's all for today." He got up, edged toward me; he seemed so anxious to get me out of his office that I wouldn't have been surprised if he had grabbed my arm and pulled me out into the hall.

On my last birthday Tom was in Minneapolis, at a conference.

I compiled the lists as instructed. Under Tom, for instance, I wrote "loyalty — mine," "companionship," "his paycheck." Under David: "passion," "conversation," "his work — I resonate." In the end the lists were virtually equal in number and substance; they canceled each other out. I went back to see Dr. Casell a few times, then quit, having thanked him and feeling that it had not been a complete waste of time — at least I had reduced my problem from a whirlwind to something that would sit still for a few minutes. I considered talking some more to Alicia Baer. But I suppose the thing that made me want to be by myself so much had come from the same place as my reluctance to bother my next-door neighbor with my problems, especially since all around us things seemed to be coming apart, wars erupting all over the globe as if peace itself was the menace.

In spite of everything, I managed to keep on working, illustrating another book for

David, a book for six-to-eight-year-olds about a little girl who wanders away from her family's vacation cottage and into the woods nearby, where she meets several animals who talk to her and teach her how to live off the land. Eventually, of course, she wanders back, happier but wiser. The story, incorporating an ounce or two of terror, was a cut above the usual drivel. Meanwhile, David bombarded me with e-mails, sometimes several a day. Sometimes he sent jokes. All the jokes were funny. I added that to his list: "great sense of humor." He sent weird pictures of George Bush, one looking through binoculars with the lens caps on. Other times the messages were personal: "I keep thinking of our shrine in the Rhinelander." I assumed he was trying to be cryptic, having taken to heart the warnings about privacy on the Internet. But anyone with half a brain could have figured that one out. I put something on Tom's side: "good judgment." Almost every night I dreamed about David. Sometimes in the dream David didn't look anything like the real David, but I knew it was him. He was very tall, with blond curly hair. He had a mustache and wore a striped suit. He was twelve years old and carried a fishing rod, like Tom Sawyer. He was an old-fashioned doctor with a long white coat — all David. In every dream we shared passionate kisses, then engaged in steamy sex. Sometimes I woke up and realized that I had had an orgasm while dreaming.

Beth too sent me e-mails, though not so often as David. My affection for this method of communication deepened and I wondered how we all managed before the Internet. Instant talk, love, attitude, assurance. Beth was getting along "okay." This probably meant that disappointment had colored her life black. Otherwise she would have sounded enthusiastic. I asked her what she did all day. It seems that a good deal of time was spent either breaking up fights or trying to get the kids "off their asses" to do some work. The food was "crappy" (what had she expected?). And among the other so-called counselors, she had made only one friend. The rest were "losers." I sighed for her, hoping at the same time that she would get fed up with the job and come home where she belonged. As for Mark, this kid amazed me: he sailed through life as if it were a constant lark, laughing off things that would have sent other people reeling — being fired, having his apartment broken into and half his stuff stolen, a speeding ticket for two hundred dollars. Nothing seemed to cloud his sunny disposition. He came to the house for dinner several times a month, often with a girl in tow, never the same one twice. He usually brought me something he'd picked up at one of the neighborhood food shops. How had he come by his wonderful ballast? Not from me, certainly.

CHAPTER 8

Does inertia trump denial, or does it work the other way around? A mildly engaging question if you have nothing better to do than split hairs, but why ask it since both denial and inertia put you in the same, morally limp place.

On a sun-drenched morning in April, while I was loading the dishwasher after breakfast, Tom sat at the kitchen table, drinking his third cup of coffee, when he said, "Dannie, there's something you and I have to talk about." For any collector of ominous phrases, this ranks right up there near the top.

"Well," I said, not turning around to face him and talking over my shoulder, "we haven't really talked much for — how many weeks? I'd say four or five at least. What do you have in mind?"

I guessed what was coming but I didn't want to make it easy for him; I wanted him to squirm and, in this, he obliged me. "I think, that is, I'm sure that our future together went off the tracks sometime last year. I don't know what happened, but we seem to have lost whatever it was that used to keep us connected. Damn, I don't know how to say it."

"Let me try," I said. "Our marriage has ground to a halt. Fuel tank's on empty. No more water in the well. Whatever." And even as I tried to be clever, I was reeling from the blow that seemed unexpectedly brutal. Hadn't I been aching to exchange Tom for David for weeks now? But having Tom say I'm through first left me sprawling, with him standing over me, a broad smile of triumph on his face. I wanted it both ways: I wanted the cake and I wanted to eat every last crumb. What was I thinking? Who has it both ways? And while I was sure he knew nothing about David — chiefly because he didn't care enough to wonder about my trips to New York, my distracted behavior — in less than a minute I had joined the company of abandoned wives. Or, not so pretty, dumped. Tossed, along with the broken lamp, the burned-out toaster, the collapsed deck chair. The damaged wife sits on a shelf in the swap shop at the dump waiting for someone to notice her and bring her home and fix her up.

"You can't be all that surprised," he said.

"You spend more and more time in Truro, I'm here by myself. How did you think I was managing? Or did you think about it at all?"

"Jesus, Tom, why didn't you say anything? I can't read your mind. You want me to read your fucking mind? How would I know if you never said anything? You're so focused on your work and your conferences, I thought you liked it this way. Why didn't you say anything?"

"I shouldn't have to. The way we were living isn't normal. And I can tell you I don't appreciate the way you're talking to me!" His cheeks were getting blotched, turning spotty with something — anger or sorrow.

"Who wants to be normal?" I said this in a voice louder than I had intended, and having turned to face him, I realized that he was actively suffering. Tears had started down across his cheeks and his hands were twisting the paper napkin as if it were a tiny neck.

"I thought maybe things would be better when you came home this time, from Truro, but they haven't — they've gotten worse. What more can I say?" He got up from the table and started to climb the stairs to the second floor. I followed him into our bedroom.

"May I ask you something?"

"Of course," he said.

"Does this have to do with what's-her-name, your little kiss-ass student — or would this have happened anyway?" It had come to me better late than never that Tom had a girlfriend and her name was probably Judith.

"What's-her-name's name is Judith Levy. Maybe you won't believe me, and I wouldn't blame you if you didn't, but this was probably inevitable. Judith happened to come by at the right time." While we talked, he "packed." That is, he was shoving underwear and other essential items into a duffle bag. "Where are you going?" I said.

"I'm not sure yet. I may eventually move in with Judith. She's got a condo in the South End. Plenty of room." How effing convenient for him. What was Judith doing with a condo in Boston when she lived in Philadelphia? This maneuver must have been in the works for quite some time.

Tom straightened with a small effort, a small grunt. He looked around our bedchamber as if it were a hotel room and said, "I'm sure you'll find someone quickly. Maybe you have already?"

"You men think a woman can't live

without a man. What makes you think I want to find someone?" That seemed to leave him baffled. "I just assumed," he said.

"Please don't assume anything. I stopped assuming anything to do with you a long time ago." I was fangs and bristles. His leaving erased, in one swift moment, all the good things we'd done and had together. If the last thing you taste is bitter, then your entire past seems bitter.

"I'll come by for the rest of my stuff later," he said. "Don't worry about anything."

I considered that a truly patronizing remark, a remark he had no right to make. "I'm having a hard time not throwing something at you."

"Please don't be so angry," he said. "It's not all that easy for me either."

"You could have fooled me," I said, my inventory of ill will and fury filling up faster than it was emptying. "You really are a prick," I said.

"I think it's time for me to split." He scribbled something on the pad next to the phone. "Here's where you can reach me — should you have to."

An hour or so after Tom left the house (during which time I sat down in the living room and tried to put myself back together

197

again), I called Raymie, while strangely light-headed, as if this couldn't be happening. My reaction to Tom's leaving reminded me of September 11, a year and a half earlier, the unrealness of it, the sudden, hideous theatricality. This when the bogus turns out to be real but also more demanding than human understanding can absorb.

When I called Raymie to tell her what had happened, she said, "You can't be exactly caught off guard, can you?"

"It's the shock," I said.

"It'll take a while," Raymie said. "Then you'll get on with your life."

"What is my life?"

"Whatever you make it," she said.

"I'm too old," I told her as shame began to melt into self-pity.

"If this was the Middle Ages, you'd be dead. It's two-oh-oh-three, so you have the chance to live maybe another thirty years. Find yourself a guy and —"

"Raymie!" I said, interrupting. "How can you say that? Tom hasn't been gone an hour and you're already suggesting a substitute. How do I know I want to live with another man — who'll turn out to be just another prick?"

"Not all men are pricks," Raymie said.

"May I ask you something?"

I told her to go ahead.

"Do you know what happened to make him leave?"

"Judith Levy. That's what happened."

"What's she got that you don't have?"

I said I didn't know, except she didn't seem to have the requisite number of scruples.

"Did Tom ever ask you not to stay in Truro alone so much of the time but to spend more time in Watertown with him? Did he ever tell you he was lonely?"

"No."

"Well, he told me."

I thought about what Raymie had said for quite a while after I hung up the phone. Two things inflamed me: (1) What made her say this? and (2) Had Tom really confided in her, or was she making it up? How come she had never said anything before? Friendship was not so clean-cut after all. What does a friend owe you more of — truth or comfort? And look what Raymie had hooked up with. A man with the sensibility of a sea slug. I called David.

"My husband walked out on me," I said, trying hard not to sound the way I felt.

"Well," he said, his voice neutral.

I told him I wasn't sure why I was calling

him. He suggested that I didn't like being alone all that much. "It's my pride," I said. "Tom and I haven't had a conversation in months. Unless you count 'Where's my other sock?' and 'I won't be home for dinner.' "

"Please don't ask me to comment," David said. "You know how I feel about you."

As for me, I felt cold. Cold in soul, body, spirit. A chill set my teeth on edge. David seemed, at that moment, irrelevant. He must have sensed this because he asked me if I was all right. I wanted to tell him that this was the stupidest question I'd ever heard, but instead I lied to him: "Someone's at the back door. Gotta go." And I cut him off in the middle of his next sentence.

My evening meal consisted of cheese and crackers and a piece of fruit, consumed in front of the television set, where I watched without seeing. When it was time for this meal, I found I couldn't swallow and ate nothing and went to bed where, surprisingly, I fell asleep quickly, trying not to feel Tom's absence as a presence. Hours later, I woke abruptly to noises in the house that I knew shouldn't be there. I began to tremble. A door closed quietly. Footsteps sounded on the carpeted stairs to the second floor, where I lay in bed, scared shitless, aware that life alone was preferable to no life at all — which I was sure I was about to forfeit to a homicidal maniac. I could scream and maybe frighten him away, but on the other hand, hearing me, he might come up and cut me up in little pieces. I forced myself to move, sit up and swing my legs over the side of the bed. Then I grabbed my robe, which I'd tossed at the foot of the bed, and struggled into it, cursing. I was so scared my teeth chattered together, click-click-click-click-click.

"Mom?"

"Beth! Is that you?" I had trouble getting the words out because my mouth had gone dry.

"Who else would it be?" she said, coming into the room. Then I lost it. I sat back down on the bed and curled into my own lap, gasping. Beth sat down beside me and put a hand on my back. "Mom? What's the matter?"

"You scared me. You fucking scared me out of my wits, Beth. I thought you were a burglar. You should have let me know you were coming home."

"I'm sorry," she said. "I just didn't want to wake you."

"What's that got to do with not warning me you were coming? You walk into a house in the middle of the night and you don't think to let anyone know you're coming. What the fuck is the matter with you?"

Beth blinked. She wasn't accustomed to this sort of vocabulary from me. I didn't care. It was time she realized it wasn't all about her. I turned on the lamp on the bedside table. In the bright light Beth looked tired, haggard, maybe sick. There was a purplish mark beneath her jawline. Her hair was a mess and her jeans were filthy.

"Please don't be angry," she said. "I didn't mean to scare you."

I uncurled myself. "Why are you here? Are you sick?"

"Can we talk about it tomorrow morning? I haven't slept in over twenty hours."

"If you must," I said. "Your bed's made."

"Where's Dad?" she asked as she headed toward the door and her room. I told her I'd tell her all about it tomorrow morning.

It took me more than an hour to calm down. Leftover terror kept me agitated and awake. Beth's sudden appearance, like her own ghost, was so startling that once, when I woke up before dawn, I thought I had dreamed the whole thing.

When I woke up for good, it was after eight. I went down the hall and peered into Beth's room. She was there in bed, her back toward me under the comforter I'd bought her years earlier. She was asleep, motionless, her clothes on the floor, the window open wide.

Beth didn't come downstairs until almost noon. I could see she had taken a shower; her hair was wrapped in a towel. The skin on her face was shiny but signs of distress lingered. Or maybe she had just developed new lines near her eyes and mouth. Time marches on, even for your baby. I think we both decided not to mention how angry I had been last night. Cheerily, I asked her what she wanted for breakfast. I was determined to treat her like a guest for twenty-four hours, at which point I would stop waiting on her. She asked for a cheese omelet, poured herself a mug of coffee and sat down at the counter. I began to put together the omelet, hyperaware of sounds: the whisk brushing the side of the bowl, the hum of the refrigerator. Closing a drawer produced a noise like a gun going off. Beth kept her chin down, not looking at me. "Where's Dad? What's up?"

I told her her father had left the house. She wanted to know why. "He doesn't want to live with me anymore," I said.

She looked at me like a fox looks at a baby chicken. For a moment I thought she was going to ask me what I'd done to him — and maybe she was, but if so, she swallowed it and asked me how long he had been gone. When I told her since yesterday morning, it must have struck both of us at the same time: she had shown up to take his place. This is nonsense, of course, but sometimes coincidence has the force of fate.

"Are you guys going to get a divorce?"

"Probably," I said. "He's got a girlfriend."

"Jesus fucking Christ," she yelled. "Why didn't I know about this? What is it with you that you keep me in the dark like a child. I'm almost thirty."

"Please don't make this any harder for me. He just left yesterday."

"But the girlfriend thing. How long has that been going on?"

"Oh I don't know, a few months."

"My God." She seemed distraught, shaking her head, getting up and walking back and forth rapidly, rubbing her face. I couldn't understand it. I could have expected surprise, but this reaction was over the top. Her father and I had finally done what almost 50 percent of married people do and she was acting as if I'd dropped Marshall into a vat of boiling oil.

"Beth, it's not the end of the world."

"Why do you keep such a big thing a secret from me? Does Mark know?"

"I don't think so."

"Honestly, Mom, you haven't done it right."

"By your lights maybe. Now suppose you tell me why you came back in the middle of the night without any warning or anything."

It felt good to lob the ball back to Beth.

"I'm going to call Dad."

I told her to go right ahead. I told her things would work themselves out, they always did. Life's little bumps, life's rough patches, pieces of broken glass embedded in a beautiful lawn, storms that uproot trees and fell power lines. Metaphors galore for the short stretch of human existence. "My God," I said finally, "you're on your own now. You can't let what we do change your life or alter your plans. It's not good for either of us, Beth."

She seemed somewhat bewildered by my vehemence. "Now suppose you tell me why you're back."

"This person, this man, one of the other staff members, well, we'd had a few beers and I guess, I don't know, I guess he thought I had something in mind I didn't have and he got a little rough."

"He raped you?"

"Almost. I screamed and someone heard me and pulled him off of me."

"You were drinking?"

"Everybody did. It was an awful place. Drugs too. The kids dealt. I guess I didn't know what I was getting into. What to say? I kept my mouth shut . . . Good omelet," she said.

"Thanks. What's that mark on your neck?"

She just looked at me and nodded. I felt terribly sorry for her. Could I have predicted something like this? Absolutely, but so what? The moral value of being right — and letting everyone know it — has always escaped me. So I was right. So what?

I told her she ought to follow up, report the guy for attempted rape. She blew off that idea: "I don't want to have to think about it," she said. I told her to take her time. She could stay here as long as she wanted. Had all this happened before, in a slightly different version?

Beth said she was upset. More about her

father leaving than about the job, which sucked anyway. "Nothing seems to happen right since September eleventh," she added.

I asked her if she thought two people ought to live together if they couldn't stand each other. But, she said, Tom and I weren't like that. I assured her we were. "Not always." I said that things and people have a way of changing so that you no longer recognize them. And please not to blame September eleventh for her miseries. "You might as well blame God," I said. "It's just as useful."

"I don't believe in God."

As I waited for Beth to regain her equilibrium, David waited for me to stop bleeding from my wounded pride. I thought it might be a good idea to tell Beth that I had a friend in New York. She understood, asked if I meant a boyfriend. He was hardly a boy, I told her, he was even older than I am. "Have you slept with him?"

"I don't think I have to answer that."

"That means you have," she said, satisfied. "I'm all right with it, Mom. You seem to forget what year this is."

I let this pass, as far off the mark as anything she'd said in a long time. "Then why did you ask?"

"I wanted to see how serious you were. Who is he?"

We were folding laundry in the basement. The walls smelled of mildew, and the light that came in through the two tiny windows above eye level was filtered through a mist of some god-awful particles I didn't especially want to know the nature of. Beth had been helping me with chores without being asked. I was a little leery of this, since it could mean she wanted to make herself indispensable to her poor old mother — and then never leave home. She had gone to see her father and had met the Other Woman, who, she reported back to headquarters, was nice-looking and bossy. "She wants things her way," Beth said. And did he seem to enjoy giving her what she wanted? Beth was certain he did. "He was grinning. She made an antipasto and focaccia from scratch. It wasn't all that good, but he said, 'Isn't this the best thing you ever tasted?'" The man was either deeply, truly in love or else physically smitten. Did it matter which? Levy could have him.

"Would you like to meet my friend?"

"Sure," she said, patting a pile of towels. "I wish we had a cat."

"Not me," I said. "I think I could persuade David to come up here for a visit."

"That's good," she said. "Mom, I've got to go now or I'll be late for my interview." She was trying for a job on a Boston-based online magazine for twenty-somethings. Part politics, part celebrity gossip. She had said, "I don't much like the sound of it. But the pay's okay. And I'm sure there are about a gazillion of us applying." I told her to go. "Break a leg."

When I spoke to David — we had already decided that he was coming to see me the following weekend — I told him Beth might not be at her most courteous. "She doesn't seem all that anxious to meet you." He told me he didn't blame her. "Why should she?" When he said this, I realized that Tom rarely, if ever, said anything that reflected a willingness to empathize. Maybe he did it inside his head, but I never heard it. And that's what counts.

"Well, if I were in her place, I certainly would."

"Don't be too sure," he said. And then we talked about other things. There were a lot of things that made me want to be with David. One was the sex, which continued to flame high, and the other was our conversations, which often went bouncing back and forth, pulling new ideas out of

209

the ether. We hooked onto each other's notions and verbal trifles in a way that was nothing like what I had done with Tom. Tom always seemed to be taking me by the hand, leading me somewhere I didn't necessarily want to go.

Change is very hard for me. When I have to make up my mind about something that will result in change (big, small, doesn't matter), I feel as if I'm up to my waist in water, trying to walk. All my life I've attempted to manage it without wild moments and without letting on what I'm going through, and I must say I've done pretty well, considering. Working often acts as a tranquilizer, blocking out the storm that inevitably accompanies change, but you can't work all day and all night. I spent more time with my next-door neighbor, Alicia, who didn't seem to mind my talking about myself, partly because I usually punctuated the complaints and worries with mockery and digs at myself so I wouldn't sound like a victim. I hate victims. Alicia might have been glad for the company of a woman herself, even though she was the kind of person who seemed to have limitless supplies of what my father used to call "self-reliance," a concept he got from having read Emerson as a prep school student in the thirties. Alicia went to movies by herself in the afternoon. She went to the South Shore to bird-watch, carrying her lunch in a backpack. She took yoga and practiced it. She went to look at the Grand Canyon by herself. She had the backbone I wished I had.

A few mornings later, while Alicia was sitting in my kitchen drinking coffee and knitting something large and colorful for a grandchild who had not yet arrived, the phone rang. It was Tom, calling to find out if I had seen a lawyer yet. I asked him what the hurry was. "Judith and I would like to get married. But we'll have to wait until you and I are divorced. It's no-fault in Massachusetts, so I don't expect there'll be much wrangling."

"So long as I get the Truro house," I thought but did not say. I wanted this stipulation to come out of the mouth of my lawyer. "I've talked to a lawyer over the phone," I said. "I have an appointment with her on Friday."

He wanted to know her name. "Why do you want to know?"

"Just asking. Old habits." For a moment I thought he was going to say "Let's call the whole thing off." There was that catch in his voice, preliminary to a good cry.

Sentiment comes so easily when you don't have to do anything about it.

"Her name is Jessica Green. She went to Stanford Law School and she's got two kids."

"I see. Well."

"Well what?" I said.

"Well, I better get back to work. I'll see you later."

Beth actually landed the job and began to do some of the same sort of things she had done at *Scrappy* but she didn't appear to mind it as much. Maybe she was just relieved to be out of her last job. From what she let drop, she was dating several men, one at a time of course, but when I asked her who they were and what they did for a living, she gave me only minimal information, as little as she could without actually telling me to go fuck myself. I suggested she get her own place and she said that she'd been looking but was thinking of moving in with Hugh. "Who's Hugh?"

"A friend." She said she was going to Market Basket and did I want anything, and this triggered something that I'd forgotten: the book we were going to do together. I mentioned it and Beth brightened. "Really?" she said. "You want to do a book with me? I'd forgotten all about it." She postponed her trip to the market and we sat down together and took notes on what we wanted to accomplish. The real true thing. Shacks and houses a notch or two above these. By the way, when had houses become homes? No one says "house" any-more. Home for sale, not house. A house is a thing with a door and a chimney with smoke coming out and flower beds in front. A home is a concept, an abstraction. "You and I are going to do houses, not homes."

Beth said, "How about for the last page we show one trophy house, the biggest and ugliest we can find. And print that without any text or caption. Just this big, stark, hideous thing blocking out the sky. Sort of like an atomic explosion."

"You're a genius," I said.

"Do you think David's publishing house would do it?"

This was the first time Beth had said his first name without giving it some kind of edge. I told her I thought it was hard to find a publisher for books of photography because they were expensive to produce and didn't have that large a market. "The glitziest ones are called coffee-table books. Which means you put them out on the

Bombay table where they reflect the sun coming in through the French windows across the immaculate lawn. Nobody really looks at them."

"They'll look at this one," Beth said. "It makes a political statement. No glitz."

Sensing Beth's excitement, I didn't want to let her see my own in case this ended in failure before it even got started. I told her I'd talk to David about our project and then reminded her that this book would take a good deal of work, a lot of just driving around the Lower Cape, back roads, etc., and looking and taking notes. Then there'd be the actual shoot, rolls and rolls of film, the light just right. And the text itself. She would have to get the tone right too. Did we want to do interiors as well as exteriors? And if we did, would we want a chronicle of the house's inhabitants over the years? Many questions, many possible problems.

"Mom," she said, "I really want to do this."

"Me too, pet."

She went off to the market, with a list from me, and I e-mailed David. "Does your house do books of photographs?"

He e-mailed back: "Sometimes. Why?"

"Just asking. How's Rudy?" He had

named his penis after the rigid and heroic mayor of New York City.

"Longing for thee," he said. "When am I going to see you?"

"Very soon I hope. Beth and I have something in mind." I didn't want him to see it until it had some professional polish. I was glad I didn't have an agent; I didn't want to deal with David through a third party. Beth and I had decided to hit the road, so to speak, the following Saturday. David asked me how I was coming along with the latest book he had sent me to illustrate. I wanted to do pictures that children would remember because they had some frightening element in them, or something baffling. This was much harder than pretty. Pretty was a snap. Menacing used every drop of imagination I had. I felt as if I hadn't moved forward in my line of work for years. Same old thing: cute children with wide eyes and determined chins. High self-esteem was an important element. Parents are hooked on self-esteem; it's today's dimples. Having begun to go stale on illustrating, I looked to the house project to take over.

Jessica Green, my nice lawyer, assured me I would get the Truro house. She had talked to Tom's lawyer and it seemed that he was not only willing but eager for me to have it. "Seems he just wants out. The woman he's living with — Levy is it? — appears to have some money of her own. Isn't that convenient?"

And what about the Watertown house? Tom's lawyer suggested we sell it and split the proceeds. Beth didn't like this idea, and neither did Mark. It was not only their house but their home, even though Mark hadn't lived there for years. I told them they could have my half of the money from the sale, but that didn't make a dent in their opposition. I told them I had decided. "You two rent a couple of U-Hauls and take what you want. It's yours." I acted as if getting rid of the house was no more difficult to me than putting a stained carpet out on the street for the trash people to pick up. I was heartbroken, the house having become precious now that it was going to be snatched away and put on the market. What stranger would sleep in the bedroom, drink coffee in the morning in the kitchen, sweep the front steps, clean the closets, set the table for eight in the dining room and light candles? Who would stand at the sink and look at the trees, bonelike in winter? Who would hang what hideous clothes in my closet, put on a skirt

216

and look in the mirror, asking herself if she looked fat? Who wouldn't sweep the basement floor? Who would open the front door to welcome her children or grandchildren with a tight hug, then follow them into the warmth inside and shut the door behind her? I couldn't stand thinking about it.

"Where are you going to live?" Beth said.

"I don't know," I said. "The Truro house."

"Not all winter," Beth said. "You'll start drinking."

"Not me," I said. "That's not my thing. I'll find plenty to do." What I wasn't telling them was that I had almost made up my mind to move to New York and share David's apartment. I don't really know why I transformed my plans into secrets to be kept from my children. Why did I do it? Partly because I sensed — in Beth at least — a strain of resistance to most of what I did. It was like a tic: Mom says A, Beth insists on B. Except for our joint project — that had an alphabet all its own.

It turned out that this Hugh person was married — though separated from his wife. I figured that maybe that made him safe to be with — no threat to her independence from men. She kept making excuses for us not to meet, which meant, of course, that she was — what? Ashamed of him? Afraid I wouldn't like him and tell her so? Afraid he would say something "inappropriate"? I called Mark and asked him if he had met Beth's new "roommate." He said he had, once, briefly. "Seems nice enough. A little geeky if you ask me." Was I surprised — I'd had him figured as a stud. Did it make any difference?

On a gray, chill day late in April, Beth and I drove to the Cape. I was not at my most serene, having run a tag sale on the sidewalk in front of our house. (My mother, in Florida, would have had a fit. Largely ignorant of many of the earth-shaking events of the last twenty years, including the events of September 11, which she refused to admit was more than a minor accident with a couple of "poor souls" dispatched by the flames, she existed inside a transparent shell that let in only the sunny hours. Why disabuse her?) The tag sale, which grossed and netted the same amount, namely eight hundred-plus dollars, had taken a lot out of me. Off in the arms of strangers went a silver tea service, a set of crystal wineglasses still in the box they came in, a blackboard from

Mark's childhood room, three cartons of books, and scores of other items I had no room and/or need for. But it hurt to see them go nonetheless. You have fewer things, you're less of a person, right?

We got off straight and boring Route 6 after we crossed the Sagamore Bridge and took instead Route 6A, which meandered its way through small towns like Yarmouthport and Dennis. These are hardly swinging towns, but largely white enclaves, not of the rich so much as of the old and careful and patriotic. I was surprised to see how many American flags there were — not the big stuck-in-the-ground kind but more discreet, on mailboxes and in windows. To be honest, I had bought a flag pin shortly after September 11 and had worn it until George Bush and Donald Rumsfeld began to scare me with their angry elephant noises. We wanted to find an unoccupied house so we wouldn't have to deal with its owners. Taking a narrow paved road off 6A on the bay side, we drove for about five minutes when Beth said "Stop!"

We were abreast of just what we were looking for: a weathered, shingled saltbox with one chimney, a brick path, a few trees that looked as if they had grown up there, not bought at a nursery, and shutters, trim and front door of the proper Cape gray-blue. "Is it too perfect?" I said. "I don't want our book to look like a calendar."

Beth got out of the car with her note-book and pen and started to take notes. I followed her with my camera and my bag of equipment. The thing was, I was sure, to find one flaw in what looked to be a Cape Cod Chamber of Commerce dream house and focus on that. The beetle crawling up the side of a mound of apples and pears in a still life. Beth had disappeared around the side of the house when the front door opened and a woman's face appeared in the crack.

"May I ask what you're doing here? This is my property and I'm afraid you're tres-passing."

The woman to whom the face belonged had steely gray hair held in place by a black band, a square jaw, and glasses on a cord around her neck. She was wearing a Fair Isle cardigan and a pleated wool skirt that hung past her knees. She had on flat brown shoes with laces. She might have been pretty had she smiled. I suppose I was gaping.

"I need to know what you're doing here." It sounded more like an instruction than a question.

"I'd like to take a picture of your beautiful house."

"That's all very well, but why do you want a picture? Do you work for the *Times*?" I assumed she meant the *Cape Cod Times*. At this point, she was standing at the top of the two curved brick steps that led to the front door.

I told her that I thought this was one of the best examples of Cape Cod architecture and that I was planning a book of photographs.

She asked me if I had a publisher and I had to tell her "not yet."

"In that case I'm afraid I'm going to have to ask you not to take any pictures. I'm sure you understand."

I didn't understand and my face must have registered this lack of comprehension.

"I have nothing against you personally, I simply can't let a perfect stranger start snapping pictures of my house."

"My daughter . . ."

"What daughter?"

"My daughter. She went around to the back of the house. We thought it was empty."

"That was a mistake. What made you think that? Because there's no car in the driveway?"

She began to follow me down the path, slowly, but with the moral force of a rhino. I called Beth who, for whatever reason, took her time coming around the side of the house. "Meet the owner," I said.

"Hi," Beth said. "Great grape arbor."

"Thank you, dear," she said.

I pulled Beth by the arm. "We're leaving," I said.

We got into the car as quickly as we could. Beth wanted to know why "that old crock" had been so pissy. "In my line of work people would kill their mothers to get their house's picture taken," Beth said.

Since I tend to view things as omens, I began to get that discouraged feeling but promised myself I could shake it off. "She was a mutation," I said. "Before we get discouraged, let's look for another house."

"What was her problem?"

"Xenophobia. Hatred of strangers. Maybe she thought we were Arab terrorists or something."

Beth began to muse out loud about how people seemed on the edge — and some of them right over the edge — of madness. It had all happened, she insisted, since September 11. She kept coming back to that, as if civilization had cracked, like a dry twig, setting people and events off in wild spinning. I told her it was just some Puritan woman with panic in her chest, not to make a big deal of it, even as I thought she had a point there, she had a point. Nothing since September 11 was wholly familiar, everything skewed, change coming faster than a tornado, the ends of the circle no longer meeting.

CHAPTER 9

It wasn't as if I believed that something would happen so that I could hold on to my house. I was long past that stage. But the people who bought it! I don't know why I minded so much. The house belonged to them now, they were paying for it. And what they paid in 2003 was three times as much as Tom and I had paid for it twenty years or so earlier. Still, you realize that when you have to let something go, money doesn't figure into it; money is the last thing you think about. *Candid Camera* once asked people on the street who were walking their dogs how much money they wanted for the dog. A raggedy woman holding a leash at the other end of which was a dog as raggedy as she was said, "I wouldn't take nothing."

Mr. Funt said, "A hundred dollars. Five hundred?" The woman kept shaking her head. Funt worked his way up to a million. The woman still shook her head. "She ain't for sale." I know what she was thinking: would you sell your child?

The closer I came to having to move out, the more I loved my house. I had a shark agent, Francine Schweitzer, an "associate" from one of the high-end agencies that do very well in the Boston area. She drove a new Lexus and wore high heels and silk scarves. She brought me a plastic bag and handed it to me. "Simmer this on the front burner." I asked her what was in it. "Sweet spices. Star anise and cloves and other good stuff. It makes the house smell heavenly. Are you sure you don't want a fluffer?"

"What's a fluffer?"

"She goes around your house fluffing pillows and generally disguising the rough spots. Sometimes she moves the furniture around." I told her I could fluff my own pillows.

"I think you're making a mistake," she said, examining the windowsill in the front room where Marshall had scratched off the paint.

"You mean if I have some stranger come in here and smooth the bedspread and sweep up a few crumbs that I'll get a better price on the house?" Francine told me I'd better believe it. "It's what everyone does. And by the way, put those family pictures of yours away for the time being." I asked her why. "When they're trying to decide whether or not to buy a house, folks don't want to see other people's smiling children and black-and-white ancestors in *their* house."

I offered her a cup of tea — which she accepted, slipping out of her shoes and draping her scarf over her chair. "That really hits the spot," she said. "Is it decaf?"

Francine had asked me to leave the house whenever she brought prospective buyers to look at it, saying that the owners were apt to trail the client, explaining things. It was a distraction. I promised I wouldn't do that. But she insisted so I agreed. She'd call me from her office suggesting I take a walk around the block or go to the movies. Usually, I went next door and visited with Alicia Baer, whom I liked more than ever now that I wouldn't be seeing much more of her. But Alicia wasn't always at home and by the second week — "We have some nibbles but no bites as yet. Don't give up, honey, this is a great property. We won't go down in price for another couple of weeks" — I began to feel like an alien in my own house. I asked Francine if they were allowed to open drawers and closets. "Not drawers. But closets and cabinets," she said. "Wouldn't you do that if you were thinking of buying a house?"

But they were staring at my things! My too many pairs of shoes and the crawl space on the third floor, crammed with old suitcases and broken picture frames, and the kids' forgotten toys and games, along with the detritus of decades. Maybe I ought to burn the place down and collect the insurance. Alicia was a definite plus. She assured me that next to death and divorce and losing a job, moving was the most stressful of human activities. "And you've got two of them."

"All I need is a death."

"Have some wine. It'll chill you out."

I told her that the day before, Francine had shown up with a couple before I had a chance to leave the house. "Well, to be honest, I didn't want to leave. Francine was surprised and asked me what I was doing there. I told her I was just about to leave. But I didn't, you see, and she couldn't very well start hassling me while these people were listening. And just as I expected, they didn't just look, they snooped. I was trailing them, I admit, but not explaining anything. Furtively, the woman opened the junk drawer in the kitchen, a room they hated. The woman called it 'god-awful.' They were discussing how they'd rip out a wall and put in a — get this — 'guest lavatory.' Have you ever used the word 'lavatory'? Well me neither. I was steaming."

"If Matisse bought your house, you'd hate him too."

She was right. It didn't matter who bought it; it was the idea of shedding it. "I'll try to be more philosophical about this," I said. "But you should have heard them. They'll take this lovely old place and 'modrenize' it. They'll rip out the stove, tear down the walls, paint the bathroom purple and lay down wall-to-wall carpeting. They'll do everything I hate. By the way, Matisse would leave it pretty much as it is. Except maybe he'd freshen up the paint."

The sale eventually went through without any major problems. I had to sit in Francine's Cambridge office with the new owners. Their names were Edward and Phyllis Nissen and their two children: Edward junior — called, of course, Teddy; and Samantha — called, of course, Sammie. At the house, Sammie had opened the cookie jar and helped herself to a couple of Fig Newtons. When I left off trailing them, the children were arguing about which one of them would get the best room.

It wasn't until I handed over the keys that I realized the Nissens were about the same age Tom and I were when we bought the house and that their children were the same ages as mine. I don't want to make too much of this coincidence. But it did bring home in an especially acute way the accuracy of *plus ça change* . . . Phyllis was me, Ted was Tom, etc., and instead of making me more miserable, the parallels seemed to cheer me up, reminding me of circles and cycles, the inevitable, whatever promise the future held.

I put most of my furniture and other stuff in one of those awful "self-storage" holding pens and moved out to Truro. It was late winter — cold, damp, with a biting wind. David came up for two weekends; his visits warmed me more efficiently than a cast-iron stove. He spent a good deal of time pleading with me to marry him. I said, "I want to see how we are at living together before I decide."

"Well, then, when are you going to join me in my lonely apartment?"

Two months later, Tom and Judith Levy married. For some reason that I will never be able to understand, the *New York Times*' Vows column covered their wedding. This was the story, verbatim.

When Judith Anne Levy came to the Massachusetts Institute of Technology in the fall of 2002, she wasn't thinking of much more than her determination to make the most of her Knight Fellowship, a prestigious and competitive award made to ten science writers from all over the United States, chosen for their specific skills. Ms. Levy is a forty-nine-year-old divorced woman with what her friends characterize as the resolve of an astronaut-in-training. "As a matter of fact, when I was growing up, I wanted to be one of the first female astronauts," she admits with a laugh. "I was nearsighted." No one would ever think of applying this condition to her drive to become a writer on such mind-twisting subjects as string theory, bioterrorism, and, lately, the social anthropology of diasporas. It was in MIT's department of anthropology that she met Thomas Faber, a professor known to his students as a tough grader and independent thinker — he's a member of the Libertarian Party, but, as one student put it, "He's a really cool guy." Faber was separated from his wife.

The professor remembers his first view

of Ms. Levy: "I didn't know who this person was, sitting in on my class on naming rites and rituals. But there she was in the back of the room, taking notes and occasionally looking out the window. I guess I noticed her pretty quickly."

"Well, sometimes I got restless, not being able to talk," Ms. Levy recalls. "But very soon I was totally involved in the class and felt like I wanted to know the teacher better." For their first date, Faber took Ms. Levy to a Bruins hockey game at Boston's spanking new FleetCenter, which replaced the legendary Boston Garden. "I think he wanted to show me he was an all-around kind of person." Levy, who grew up in a suburb of Philadelphia and graduated from Wellesley College, has a master's degree in communications from Johns Hopkins University.

Ms. Levy dated several other Boston men. "Tom was still married. Who knew what would happen?" she said philosophically. But the divorce came through sooner than she had even hoped. And that was the end of "meeting guys for coffee at Starbucks and listening to them talk about themselves. Tom was different: His mind zipped all over the place. He knows rap and grand opera. He loves movies and he cooks!"

Last May 11, Levy and Faber were married at the Columbia Faculty Club by Rabbi Sarah Ginzburg, a cousin of the bride's, assisted by L. Philip Granger, associate minister of Trinity Church in Copley Square. Professor Faber says, "You know, I used to think you had to be Jewish to eat rye bread. Now I know that anyone can eat rye bread and that to be Jewish is to have a heart as big as Judith's. Honestly, I wasn't looking for anyone, not at my stage in life, but well, you know the rest of the story." The couple, who have been living in Ms. Levy's condo overlooking Boston's waterfront, chose to marry in New York because it represented a spatial compromise between the bride's home in Philadelphia and the groom's in Boston.

The bride's college roommate and closest friend, Mary Singer, says, "Everyone envies Judy her perfect skin and her high I.Q. She's a winner."

Mark Faber was his father's best man. His daughter Beth, a budding writer, was there, as she put it, "with bells on." "We're thrilled for Dad," she said. "Judy's the perfect match for our old man."

The ceremony, attended by several

dozen of the bride's and groom's old and new friends, was short on religion and long on the kind of vows that attest to the couple's singular creativity. Ms. Levy read a passage from *The Double Helix*, James Watson's book about the helical structure of DNA; Professor Faber chose a section from anthropologist Ruth Benedict's work *Patterns of Culture*. The rabbi beamed at the couple under a Huppah fashioned from bamboo shoots and green chiffon — "the color of hope," Ms. Levy explained.

After the ceremony, the couple and their friends moved on to the reception. There, amid a forest of plants, tables sparkled with glitter and palm fronds. "It was Beth's idea," Ms. Levy said. "She was my invaluable assistant." A message from the bride's mother, who was unable to come up from Florida because of a recent fall, was read. "My darling girl has my every blessing. She deserves this happiness — now if she would only learn to cook kugel for her new husband, my life would be complete." The message brought down the house.

Professor Faber's longtime friend Grant Barnes, an attorney from Cleveland, told us that he'd been worried for some time about his friend: "He didn't seem like he

233

needed anyone to be there for him, you know, in good times and bad. Then this wonderful person comes along, and Tom's an absolute goner. They just love each other to pieces."

The couple won't take a honeymoon immediately but plan to travel to the Marquesas in July. "The dream of my life," Professor Faber said, "except that now I will share it with my dream of a woman." Ms. Levy beamed.

David was on the phone to me before I could call him. "Have you seen it?" he said.

"It made my skin crawl," I told him. "I didn't want to read it all the way through but I made myself. Would you like me to deconstruct it for you? How much time do you have?"

"Will it make you feel better?"

"I don't know. I hope so."

He told me to go ahead. It was very nice of him.

In the first place, I told him, they got Judith's age wrong. I happened to know that she was closing in on fifty-one. I thought the *Times* had fact-checkers. Secondly, we were not "separated" when they met. We were still living in the same house and hadn't yet admitted that our marriage was about to go south. That woman just lied to the reporter. As for his taking her to a hockey game, that was so much crap. "He's never been to a hockey game in his life." David said maybe she had changed him. "People don't change," I said. "They just get older." I was annoyed. It sounded to me as if he were taking their side.

"Whose side are you on?" I said.

"Nobody's. I'm just listening. Why do you think he took her to a hockey game?"

"Beats me," I said. "Maybe it's his way of getting back at me." As soon as I said this, I realized how silly it sounded.

"Go on," David said.

"Tom knows rap the way I know Sanskrit. What is she *talking* about?"

"You know, Dannie, you shouldn't believe most of the stuff in that column. It's mostly made up."

"David, it isn't!"

"I'm exaggerating. But the Vows column isn't where you go for information. It's where you go for a romantic story. There's a difference."

I asked him if he wanted me to continue. He said only if I really needed to. I could tell he was uncomfortable with my whining — because that's what it was. The part of the story that really hurt my feelings was about Beth and Mark. What they hadn't said — or what it was reported they hadn't said — was that either I had never existed or had been a terrible wife for Tom. How could they? They had both told me about having gone to their father's wedding, but you wouldn't know, from what they said about it, that it was the same event as the one described in the *Times*, not so much the facts but the tone and style. According to them, it was very low-key and the rabbi had gone on and on and on until people started coughing and scratching. Grant Barnes — whom incidentally I had heard Tom mention only once or twice in the entire time we were married — got plowed and came on to Beth like a satyr, then fell down and passed out on the floor. Judith was chilly to them, or, as Beth put it, "She's always on," as if she thought everyone was watching her and listening to her. "She's the most artificial woman I've ever met. I don't know what Dad sees in her."

Reading the Vows account of my husband's wedding, it occurred to me that the truth lay somewhere in the middle, between that account and that of my children who, bless their hearts, only wanted me to be cool and generous and, above all, unwounded.

I told David I missed him and he asked me again when I was coming to New York to live with him. "I need you terribly," he said.

So I went. Although it killed me, I loaned Marshall to Beth, who said she wouldn't mind keeping him so long as I paid for his food and medical expenses. I made her promise to walk him at least once a day and not to feed him scraps from her plate. I moved into David's place on Twelfth Street. It was strange enough relocating to a city I barely knew, but living with a man I didn't know much better, having perceived him mainly under the rosy glow of desire, I wasn't prepared for the real man who soon emerged. My original take on him — that he was nice and honest and unpretentious and interesting and occasionally humorous — didn't change, but I began to notice that he had several unattractive habits, just like the rest of us. For instance, he talked before he finished chewing and swallowing his food; sometimes bits of potato or soup or lettuce clung to his lips. How was it that I had never noticed this before? I can only guess that it was because I didn't want to. He spent thirty-five or forty minutes every morning taking a shower and God only knew what else. He wasn't one of those people who are casual about privacy. When the door was closed, it was understood that I wasn't supposed to open it. Whenever the phone rang and he answered it, he always cleared his throat three times. Does this sound as petty as I think it does?

I have plenty of habits I'd rather not have and he never mentioned them, so I'll add tact to his plus column. He never said anything about the way I always checked more than once or twice things like: Had I left a stove burner on? Was the door double-locked and bolted? Did I have my keys? He never said anything about my insistence on washing up after dinner no matter how tired I was or how horny he was. We none of us are easy to live with if you let these and even worse habits get under your skin, where they swell to enormous size.

One Sunday morning while I lay in bed listening to the sounds on the street — cars driving by the house, a piercing whistle, the thud of the *New York Times* hitting the stoop — and trying to decide what to do today, I heard David yell "Oh shit!" from the kitchen. I called, asking him what was the matter. "I cut myself!"

I ran into the kitchen, where I saw David standing over the counter. Blood dripped from his hand onto the clean white surface. He turned around and looked at me ruefully. "I was cutting this bagel," he said, holding it up. It was pink. "Let me see your hand," I said.

"It's nothing."

"It's not nothing, look how it's bleeding. At least put some pressure on it. Hold it under the cold water tap."

David's face was turning ashy, whether from the pain, blood loss, or fear, I couldn't tell. "Please let me see it, David." He held out his left hand. The index finger was badly cut. You could see the bone inside the knife cut. My knees buckled slightly and I held on to the counter. "You need to get that sewn up," I said. "I'll get dressed."

"No way," he said. "I'll just hold this paper towel over it 'til it stops bleeding."

"It's not going to stop by itself. It needs to be sewn." Clearly, he had not, as I had, gone through this grisly routine with children. I spent the next five minutes trying to persuade him to let a doctor take care of it. I think the fact that the bleeding did not let up was more persuasive than whatever I said to him, and he finally agreed.

We found a cab on Sixth Avenue and drove to St. Vincent's Hospital, a place that was put on alert when the Twin Towers went down, told to get ready to handle hundreds, maybe thousands, of the injured. Except that there were only two. Everyone else either walked away or died.

David and I sat in the Emergency waiting room, which featured plastic chairs, bars over the first-floor windows, and screaming babies. The triage nurse who looked at David's hand said, "You'll live," and put him in line. There were about a dozen people waiting. David kept apologizing to me, suggesting that I go back to the apartment and that he'd take a cab home when he was done.

I told him not to be ridiculous. Of course I'd stay with him. I'd sing to him if he wanted. I'd read him a three-year-old copy of *Good Housekeeping*. I found it odd that he was so apologetic. It made me wonder what his marriage had been like. Had she been someone who didn't endorse the first part of "in sickness and in health," like Ruthie Brenner? Some women freak out when something bad happens to their spouse or significant other. "Stand by your man" means as much to them as filling up the gas tank with premium. They don't want to change dressings or take the poor guy to the bathroom. They want to party.

Most of the people in the waiting room looked neither sick nor wounded except for a young woman with a terrible, dry cough and runny eyes, probably spreading germs galore. It occurred to me that Sunday is the day people go to the E.R., when they're looking for a little drama in their lives: people with wax in their ears, rings they can't remove, or a teeny little pain in the knee joint. I sat next to David, whose injured digit he had wrapped in a large, once-white cotton handkerchief. A television set mounted high up a wall was showing a cavernous "church" filled with smartly dressed white people. The preacher — it was impossible to guess his denomination — walked back and forth across what looked far more like a stage than an altar, and told his "congregation" that there was nothing wrong with earthly goods so long as they didn't interfere with their spiritual journeys. Eyes followed him raptly. I whispered something rude about them in David's ear and he nodded in a distracted way. He was not a happy camper. The handkerchief was turning pink. I went up to the desk and asked how much longer it would be until my "husband" was seen by a doctor. The woman looked up at me and said, "We're taking them in order. We'll call his name when it's his turn."

"Yes, but do you have any idea how long that might be?"

"His name will be called."

We sat there for more than three hours. When I finally heard "David Lipsett," I was too zoned to realize that meant us. David had to poke me. "Do you want to come in with me?"

"Would you like me to?"

"It's up to you."

I had the feeling he wanted me to come with him, so I did. A nurse wearing flowered scrubs took us into a large room with curtained-off areas and beds. She told David to lie down. He did so. There was no place for me to sit except on an ice-cold steel stool. In a few minutes a woman came in and introduced herself as Dr. Pierce. Should I tell her I thought Pierce was an apt name for a doctor? Apologizing, she asked me to relinquish the stool. Then she sat down, drawing an arm rest out from beneath the bed. "Now let's see what we have here." She unwrapped the handkerchief and asked him whether he wanted it back. "You can keep it," he said with a trace of a smile. She told him he looked familiar, a remark that elicited a shrug from David. "I don't think so."

"I'm going to have to take a few stitches in this. It's a pretty deep cut. You say you did it cutting a bagel?"

When she was done sewing up David's finger, she gave him a tetanus shot and told him to come back in three days to have the stitches removed.

"Let's go have lunch somewhere," I said. "I'm starving."

David thanked me again for staying there with him and being so patient. And I asked him not to thank me again. "Five times and I get the idea."

Along about this time I got a phone call from Beth, who reported that her old flame, Andrew, had appeared one night at the door of her apartment in Jamaica Plain. No warning, no telephone call, just him. I gather she was cheerful but chilly. "I asked him what he was doing here," she told me.

"You invited him in?"

"Of course," Beth said. "It was almost midnight. He set it up that way."

The woman who shares Beth's apartment, Claire, was asleep. They each have their own bedroom and use a common kitchen and living room. Claire works for a department in the State House that has to do with looking out for the welfare of children, victims of abuse, neglect, and ignorance. As a bureaucrat, she's not in danger of losing her job when there's an electoral turnover. She's nice enough but doesn't have Beth's sense of humor or spirit, due, no doubt, to the kind of woes she has to deal with every day. The two women seem to get along with a minimum of abrasion.

Beth invited Andy to come in. Marshall was barking like crazy; he never did take to Andy; I think Andy must have kicked him once when no one was looking. Andy didn't say anything much about the place, asked her if she lived alone and then tried to kiss her. She stepped back. "I knew we still had that chemistry thing," she told me, and she didn't want to see how strong the temptation was. Andy sort of shrugged it off and asked if she had any beer.

Beth told me this with a good deal of prompting on my part. I think she wanted me to know the outcome without all the details that led up to it, but I was curious to find out how she dealt with this man who had been her Svengali. One look from him was enough to make her do whatever he wanted her to. How to dress, what to eat and not eat (soup!). What music to listen to, what friends to cultivate, how to chop onions, what sort of garment to wear to bed (none!).

"I think he was sort of flummoxed to find out I was sharing the place with someone else. Then I asked him why he had come up without telling me. He admitted that maybe if he'd told me I wouldn't let him come up. But of course I couldn't have stopped him if he really wanted to see me. It was so weird, Mom, with me being the one in charge."

She let him spend the night on the couch in the living room. The next morning — it was a Saturday — the three sat around drinking coffee and eating muffins, with Claire bestowing "fishy" looks on Andy, looks which he bounced right back at her. "It was actually kind of funny," Beth said.

"Did he want something? I mean something specific?" I said.

"He wanted us to get back together." In spite of common sense, I held my breath.

"And?"

"And I told him I was no longer interested in carrying on a sick relationship with anybody. Claire got up and went back to her bedroom at this point in time."

245

"I'll bet he got nasty," I said. She asked me how I knew.

"Because people like Andy can't tolerate rejection." Beth said nobody liked it.

"Nobody likes it, but they learn how to deal with it. My God, I sound like somebody's mother!"

Among other observations, Beth said Andy told her she wasn't mature enough to keep up an adult relationship. She was a baby who would never grow up. He said she was getting fat and that soon no one would want to be seen with her. "I asked him to bring his dish over to the sink and then leave."

"And?"

"He left but he didn't bring his dish over. I guess that was showing me, right? Am I right?"

"I'm proud of you," I said.

"I'm proud of me too. Because you know what, Mom? All the time he was there, I could feel the juices flowing. I could feel my heart go a mile a minute. I guess I'll never quite get over him."

"Every woman has an Andy in her attic. Or closet."

We talked about our book. We had been taking a day here, a day there, and scouring the Cape for the kind of house we wanted to immortalize in our book. It wasn't easy because it involved a long drive for me from New York. Beth and I usually spent Saturday night in Truro. I must say, David was extremely understanding. Also very helpful; he had an instinctive feel for the way words and pictures can join hands and bring something off that seems fresh rather than a retread. Beth's text was a little edgy; she accepted nothing head-on. So that while you could tell that she admired each house for its aesthetic integrity, she also put it in a historical context. The bottom line was that these were relics, or artifacts; the only difference between them and, say, a museum of early Americana, was that people were living in them. I think she felt that maybe they ought to be wearing period dress, as at old Sturbridge Village or Plimoth Plantation. We decided not to interview the people who owned the houses but, in certain cases, to use pictures of the rooms inside.

David tried to make sure that I had a decent place to work. He suggested the back room on the ground floor, which gave out through French windows onto a scruffy, dusty patch of so-called garden. "This is the lightest room in the house," he said. At one time it had been a formal dining room with fancy sconces on the wall and a stone floor covered here and there by small rugs. I told him it would be fine but kept silent about the light — it had a southern exposure when what I need is north light. When I wasn't working on illustrations for various publishers — luck was running with me; I had more offers of work than I could handle — or taking pictures for our Cape book, David and I spent as much time together as we could. I felt younger than Beth. We went out to dinner at least once a week, not fancy restaurants, but places where the bar and the dining area occupied the same space and the food was good but not too pricey. David said you had to be a real New Yorker to know where these spots were; magazine and newspaper reviewers usually passed them over, so they had to try harder and charge less. He wanted me to walk around neighborhoods I wouldn't have visited by myself: Chelsea, site of the infamous hotel where rock star Sid Vicious slaughtered his girlfriend, thus living up to his name; the Armenian section, New York's pale emulation of Watertown; the Lower East Side, where David's grandparents had lived five flights up in a tinderbox called a tenement. David knew the building was on Hester Street but didn't know which number — how quickly our pasts are erased. He took me to Katz's delicatessen, where he ordered a tongue sandwich and a pastrami sandwich so crammed with meat that my jaws couldn't fit around it. We stood above Ground Zero, where, as at the Vietnam Memorial, I found that tears blocked speech. As we walked uptown and away from the hole, I told David I thought they ought to leave it just the way it was — what better reminder? Why try to gussy it up with sparkling new structures, a park and fountains and God knows what else? Keep it stark. David said, "How about one small headstone with a few words on it?" "Okay," I said. We went to Ellis Island; zipping around New York, he was like a high school sophomore showing off his school's new athletic facilities.

As much as I was co-opted by David's enthusiasm, the city sometimes made me gloomy. Sad little trees with limp yellow leaves and dog poop surrounding them; the dog poop reminded me of how much I missed Marshall. Buildings hid the clouds. There was constant noise that I took personally; horns, brakes, car alarms that no one paid any attention to, tires screeching, whistles, shouts, garbage trucks grinding and thrashing, sirens, glass shattering, and assorted thumps, bangs, crashes, and howls. I made David take me to the Central Park Zoo so I could hear some birds. He bought me a CD with nothing but bird sounds on it, but it only made me sadder when I listened to it. I told David I thought there were too many people in New York. "Too many? This is Mecca. This is the promised land."

"Depends on what you want," I said.

"You know, I'm almost afraid to ask you what you want."

I was thinking that maybe I didn't know what I wanted and that was the trouble. I wanted to live with David, talk to him, cook with him, go to bed with him, see his five o'clock shadow first thing in the morning. And I also wanted the minimalist life I had composed for myself in Truro. How could one person want two things so different from each other? It was like wanting to be the commanding general and AWOL at the same time. Was I trying to do something impossible?

The day I received a letter in an envelope addressed not by a lopsided sticker but by a hand holding a pen, I knew it had to contain news either very good or very bad. The letter was from an editor whose name I had heard but who I had never worked with. He overpraised my work — "the preeminent illustrator of children's stories" — and went on to inquire if I would be interested in doing the illustrations for a centennial edition of *Peter Pan*. "I am afraid," the letter continued, "that we can only pay you a flat fee of ten thousand dollars. But we plan to do a hefty promotion for this volume, as well as a special leather-bound limited edition." I ran to the phone and called David at work. "I'm really excited," I said. "How could he know how much I like Barrie? I guess I have to admit I feel very honored." "You should feel honored," David said. "I'm proud of you." Then he asked me how I was going to get this project done, along with all my other work. I told him I'd just have to work twice as hard and long. And, I added silently, "In lousy light."

Mark came down to spend a weekend with us. I hoped he had come with an open mind about me and David. After all, his father had hooked up with a new significant other so it was only fair that I do too. But I had a lingering inflammation over the way he and his sister had come off in the *Times*' Vows piece. The three of us were sitting around before dinner. I wanted

Mark to see that I wasn't waiting for him and me to be alone before I challenged him, that I considered David to be a member of the family. "Why did you tell that person that Judith was a perfect match for your dad?" David looked down into his glass of wine. Mark shuffled his big feet. "You didn't have to say that, Mark. Didn't you stop to think about what it would do to me?"

"Mom," he said, "I didn't say that. The lady asked what I thought about my father marrying Judith. I said he seemed okay with it. She put those words in my mouth. Anyway, what would you like me to say? 'This is a no-good marriage'? C'mon Mom, we were at the reception!"

"I think he's got a point?" David said.

"Who asked you?" I said, but in a voice that indicated I was joking.

"Look, Mom," Mark said. "You may hate Dad but we don't —"

"I don't hate your father," I said, interrupting.

"Whatever," Mark said. "Anyway, Beth and I would like to see him, well, maybe not happy but at least happier than he was. Same goes for you, Mom."

It was obvious Mark was trying hard to put the brightest light on everything and everybody. And I couldn't help being pleased about this. The next day David and Mark took a walk together while I prepared Sunday brunch. It turned out they had talked about the kind of music Mark plays, something I know next to nothing about. They brought me back a bunch of flowers.

Mark had got a raise at work and it seemed as if he was gradually accepting the fact that he was not going to be a rock star after all. This I took as a sign of hope. When he left, he gave me a great hug while whispering directly into my ear, "I think you got yourself a really good guy."

As soon as he closed the door behind him, David put his arms around me. I dropped my chin into the hollow just beside the bottom of his neck, a place that held my chin like a warm palm. He said that Mark was a good kid. "He knows who he is."

"Do you really think so?"

"Absolutely. You and Tom did something right."

The phone rang. David answered. "It's for you. Raymie."

"You'll never guess what Mitch and I have decided to do," she said.

"Tie the knot?"

"No, something even better."

CHAPTER 10

Raymie was just about to tell me what she had done this time when David, on the ground floor, started yelling and cursing "Oh shit, oh fuck!"

"I've got to call you back, Raymie, David's shrieking."

Pulled by the noise, I found David in his study, a room he had converted from a pantry. There wasn't much light in there — but after all, he wasn't a painter so he didn't need more than one focused lamp. He had left the old soapstone sink where it was; it was filled with papers he said he couldn't throw away. "What happened?" I said.

He was sitting on the floor, barefoot, in his bathrobe. His face was gray, his features twisted. "Oh my God," he said, "I think I broke my foot."

"How?"

He nodded toward a brass elephant paperweight. It lay on the floor on its side, as if dead. "It got me here," David pointed to his instep. The foot looked okay to me. I asked him what made him think it was broken. The pain, he said. It was really bad. Could he stand up? I offered to help him, but he shrugged me off, saying he wanted to see if he could do it by himself. Holding on to the side of his desk and groaning softly, he hoisted himself upright. He was wearing shorts and a tee-shirt under the bathrobe. I asked him what he was doing half-dressed. "I was about to take a shower," he said.

"Now?" I said.

"Why not? It's as good a time as any."

"Then what were you doing down here? The shower's upstairs."

"Do I have to file all my flight plans?" he said.

"I'm sorry. It's none of my business." He didn't dispute this point. Gingerly, he placed the injured foot flat on the floor. "Yow! I'm sure it's broken." I looked again. It still looked okay, but what did I know about how long it takes before a break turns your flesh purple? "We've got to get you to the E.R.," I said.

"It can wait 'til tomorrow," he said.

"Are you sure? Why don't you ice it and lie down?"

I fetched one of those blue things filled with a chemical that I store in the freezer for keeping sandwiches cold and chilling bruises. David was very tractable and followed me, hopping upstairs to the bedroom, where he lay down. I had wrapped the icer in a towel. Since his toes pointed upward, I had to tie the thing to his foot with the towel. He thanked me lavishly, as if I had saved him from a burning building. "Hey," I said, "I didn't do anything."

"Yes you did. You didn't get angry."

I asked him what he was talking about. "Did your mother get mad at you when you hurt yourself?"

"She'd scream at me and tell me I was a klutz," he said.

"That's terribly sad," I told him. "I want to hear more but right now I've got to call Raymie. I hung up on her when you hurt yourself."

Raymie answered the phone: "What's up?" I apologized for interrupting our conversation. "What happened?" she asked.

"David dropped a paperweight on his bare foot. He thinks it's broken."

"Ouch," Raymie said. "He should put some ice on it to keep it from swelling."

I told her I'd already done that. And now, what was her news? "Are you ready for this?" she asked.

"We'll see, won't we?" I couldn't have

guessed in a million years what Raymie told me then. "Mitch and I are going to turn part of this house into a bed-and-breakfast. What do you think of that?"

I told her I was glad I was sitting down. "You're joking, yes?"

"I'm joking, no. Here's the thing." It had started out as a semijoke, she told me, when one morning at breakfast Mitch had pointed out that each of them had been in the same racket. At first she didn't understand. "The hotel business," he'd said. The fact that he owned several glitzy, resort-type hotels — now managed by the errant son, who turned out to have a flair for running things — and Raymie had run one small B&B at the end of the earth, was irrelevant. They both had done basically the same thing, namely, made their guests happy enough so they would want to come back. They would tell their friends about the place, so they wouldn't mind — or wouldn't notice — paying a steep price for clean towels, scrubbed toilets, and halfway decent food. At this, Raymie said she objected: she actually made very little, maybe fifteen dollars on each guest, maybe not even that much. Mitch had looked at her in a way that suggested he could have nudged this net up without distressing any of the customers. It was the little things, he'd insisted, like dried flowers in an antique vase on the bureau, like real napkins at breakfast, and so on. So here they were, two middle-aged bodies, one not all that mobile, living in a house so large that Raymie admitted she had entered one of the upstairs rooms only once — to close a window that had blown open. She needed something to do; she was going nuts not doing anything but weeding the garden. She loved to cook. "Irish oatmeal, French toast, English muffins, Belgian waffles. I overheard someone," she went on, "calling this house a starter castle, and that's when I decided that Mitch had a pretty good idea." That wasn't all: she and Mitch wanted me to take the pictures for their brochure. I told her I'd never heard of a B&B doing a brochure. "So what?" she said brightly. "*We're* going to."

I told her I'd have to think about it. I was pleased that they wanted me to do the picture (how on earth do you make a house like that look warm and fuzzy?), but if I did it, it would mean abandoning my muscular — and largely useless — principles. Mitch Brenner's style — mental, physical, aesthetic — was so different from mine that I couldn't see myself working with him under any circumstances. The only reason I put up with him at all was that he was holding my best friend captive. "Not only the brochure," Raymie continued as if she hadn't heard me say that I'd have to think about it, "but we'd like you to decorate the three rooms we want to turn into guest bedrooms. You know, the best in Cape antiques — and not the kind that are going to collapse under an active couple, if you know what I mean. Good stuff, sleigh beds, canopy beds, bureaus seven feet high — sturdy but beautiful. Also the dining area. Linens, flatware, you know, the whole nine yards. We want this place to be a gem."

"The best?"

"Exactly. I haven't seen Mitch this excited since I visited him in the hospital. We'll pay you ten thousand dollars; five up front."

"That's a lot of money."

"Honey, he's got it. By the way, in case it makes you feel better, Mitch announced that he thought he might have made a mistake letting the architect talk him into building this monster house."

"He feels guilty?"

"I don't know about that," Raymie said, "but he wants more of it to be used by people who'll appreciate the quiet and the view."

Again, I told her that I would let her know as soon as I'd made up my mind.

"Don't take too long. We want to get this thing off the ground."

The next day David called his doctor, who referred him, over the phone, to an orthopedist. He told me not to come with him. "You have to work. I can do it by myself."

"What if you can't find a cab?"

"Please, Dannie, don't worry about me. I'll be fine."

While David was being tended to, I got down to work. I had one book half done and I'm afraid I bagged my usual leisurely, deliberate approach. I sketched out several ideas using a pencil and a large pad, and tried to persuade myself that I was satisfied. But haste made me feel I was short-changing the book. So what did I do? I threw everything away and started over again, having wasted three hours; I felt better and worse at the same time. The *Peter Pan* editor said he was sending me a copy of the book — it was mine to keep whether or not I decided to do the illustrations.

I hadn't told David about Raymie's proposal because I wanted to make up my mind alone, without being swayed by anyone else's agendas. So I worked on through the morning, trying not to think about Raymie's offer. Around twelve-thirty David called me on his cell phone and said he'd had his foot X-rayed and was now sitting in a little cubicle, with nothing to read but a three-year-old copy of *Popular Mechanics*. He'd been waiting for the doctor to come back with a reading of the X-ray and, presumably, a diagnosis for "half a fucking hour." Meanwhile his foot had swelled to almost twice its normal size and was turning the color of eggplant.

I rummaged through our freezer and found some lamb shanks, food that David especially liked, and started off the evening meal by defrosting and then braising them with cinnamon, allspice, and tomato paste. When David finally came home, close to five, he was encased up to the knee in a cast. Fortunately, it was the kind you could remove to take a shower. He had a pair of aluminum crutches and a sort of slipper thing on his broken foot. His expression was plaintive. "Hello, pet," he said. "I'm back from the wars. Four little bones broken. Give us a kiss."

I asked him how long he would have to be on crutches.

"About six weeks."

He made us each a whiskey and soda and sat wearily down on our living room couch, placing the crutches on the floor beside him. He stared at his broken foot — or what he could see of it. Then he beckoned me to come and sit with him. "I wish I wasn't such a goddam klutz."

I told him not to dwell on it. There was nothing he could do except maybe be a little more careful. I told him I loved him. Jimmy Stewart had fashioned a whole career out of being clumsy. Women liked this trait; it brought out the hidden mother.

During dinner David looked definitely "peak-ed" — a favorite expression of my own mother. "This is really very good," he said, pointing with his fork at the glistening lamb thigh on his plate. "But I guess I'm just not very hungry."

"Who would blame you?" I said, although I was vaguely irritated. As for me, not having eaten since breakfast, I was ravenous. "We'll have it tomorrow."

I kept waking up all during the night, almost every hour on the hour. David, having taken a pill of some sort, snored heavily beside me. I woke again a few minutes before six. I think I was seeing the first pale streaks of light in a day that promised nothing but very bad weather. I didn't want to believe it. The forecast had been so rosy.

David — funny, I never thought of him as "Dave" — had more than a little trouble managing the crutches. His foot began to ache and he wondered whether he should call the doctor. It was out of the question for him to take the subway to work as he generally did, so he would have to look for a cab — at rush hour. I suggested that he could work from home for a while, until he felt more comfortable. "What a good idea," he said. "Why didn't *I* think of that?" At this, I did a double take. Why *hadn't* he thought of it? Was I slipping into the role of — which was it, caretaker or caregiver? Although he made me glow inside and out, what price would I have to pay for this pleasure? Did I want to be his mommy?

David phoned his office and explained the situation, so that was fixed. I loved having him there — he seemed as interested in what I had to say as he had been when we first met. This amazed me, as I was used to Tom, who always seemed to be listening to me with one ear only. But the downside was that he was always in the house. Isn't that awful? I'd never quite understood what women meant when they said about their retired husbands, "He's always underfoot."

I honestly think he tried to let me work in peace, but he just couldn't help interrupting me at work to ask for my opinion about this or that — usually a manuscript he was considering, or an illustration. He also seemed blithely unaware of where certain things were stowed — in his own house! As soon as the little woman moved in, she was the keeper of toilet paper, bath soap, scratch pads, bottle opener, warm gloves. More. It's a silly list meant only to convey how helpless he thought he was. "How did you find things before I moved in?" I said, making sure my tone stayed in the light range. There it was again: How helpless can a man be? Did I truly want to find out?

"Mostly, I didn't," he said. "What would I do without you?" He came to me and kissed me on the mouth, melting my challenge. He was a great kisser. "I promise, I'll try to do better. I do love you. I feel like I'm eighteen years old and living in what my old bubba would have called 'sin.' Very exciting, really." How could I resist him, he was so even-tempered and reasonable? He never had a tantrum, didn't throw things, kept the verbal abuse at a wattage so low it burned out before it reached me. We made love at least four times a week.

Meanwhile, I embarked on the *Peter Pan* job, buoyed by having been asked to do this; it was unquestionably a plum of a job. I didn't want to make the characters cute, nor did I want them to seem like alien creatures. They were human and superreal at the same time. To get it right I tried over and over again, each time able to blur the distinction between realism and fantasy a little more. I was patient with myself.

I had several conversations with Raymie, who kept pressing me to accept her offer. And I kept pushing her deadline forward. "What does David think?" she said. "What's that noise?"

"I'm washing the dishes. I can talk and wash the dishes at the same time. David's noncommittal. He's too absorbed in his foot."

"You know, Dannie, I've been thinking about his foot thing. Is he accident-prone? Sounds like your sweetie-pie is accident-prone."

"Are you nuts?" I said, not bothering to hide my irritation. "There's something wrong with those people. They *want* to get hurt. David isn't like that."

"He isn't? How many accidents has he had since you've known him?"

I thought a moment. "Not that many. Everybody hurts themselves from time to time. I burned the top of my hand the other day."

She asked me about David's missing finger. That was when he was a little boy, I told her. You couldn't count that. I hadn't told her about the time he was almost killed by a bicycle. And I didn't say anything about it now, nor about a couple of minor mishaps of the summer before.

I assured Raymie that she would get my answer about the brochure and the rest of it in the next few days. After I hung up, I began to consider her question. Were all David's accidents really accidental, or had something he didn't want to think about made him do it to himself. This wasn't such a big deal, of course. Being accident-prone was far down on the list of human defects. One could live with it; one could even ignore it. It wasn't as if David was a crackhead or dressed in women's clothes. But it did suggest that here was someone who needed someone to watch his step for him. A man who wanted pampering and more TLC than I cared to give him. A man

266

whose mate was constantly on edge, waiting for the next blood-soaked mishap to occur. Was he merely a little needy or did the passiveness have an aggressive tail? That wasn't exactly where I had planned to go with the rest of my life. Did we communicate with each other or not? Wasn't that part of why we got along so well? Okay then, I told myself, if you're so open, just put it to him.

I was nervous. When you accuse someone of not being adult, it's not as if you were asking them why all their shirts are blue or why they never eat boiled eggs. I chose my time carefully, on a night when we went out for dinner. No big scenes in restaurants. Not that David and I had ever had a big scene, but I was aware that I might be playing with one of his rawest nerves. We had a favorite place, Cantos, a few blocks from the apartment. David was off crutches and was using a cane. We walked arm in arm.

Along about the dessert course — they had excellent lemon sorbet — I started to circle the red-hot subject, easing into it slowly, sticking one foot over the glowing coals, then withdrawing, then moving in again. I could see, by the way David's forehead was creased, that he suspected something was up. "Hey, pet, is there something bothering you?"

I said, well yes there was. Not a big thing, really, just something that wouldn't go away. Was it something about him? he asked. I nodded. "I would never make you unhappy," he said.

"I know that," I said. "I love being with you."

"Then what is it?"

"David, please don't overinterpret and please, please don't take this the wrong way."

"My God, what has the man done? Have I betrayed you? I don't think so. Have I put poison in your pasta? Have I failed to tell you I love you and that you've brightened my life?"

"Okay, okay," I said. "All those accidents?"

"What about them?"

"David, did you ever wonder why you had so many accidents?"

His face rearranged itself into a broad smile. "Is that all? Is that what you're worried about? I can't quite believe this."

I told him it worried me. The finger, the foot. The fireworks accident. How many times had he got hurt that I didn't know about? He said, "You're serious, aren't you?"

"Well, I know it sounds silly but I guess I am." The smile faded away.

"I can't believe this," he said.

Our waiter came over with two espressos. While he put these down in front of us, we went mute. I guess he was used to men and women squabbling over dessert and coffee. "We'd like our check, please," David said.

Once outside, walking back to his place, David pressed me to explain, and I have to admit that when the problem was out in the open between us, it didn't seem half so hot as it had earlier. He wanted to know exactly how much of an issue his "accidents" were for me. Rashly, I said, "It's the accidents plus, well this sounds crazy, but I think you need someone to take care of you, to sort of watch over you and make sure you're all right. Maybe you should talk to somebody."

"Talk to somebody? You mean a shrink?" The look on his face read, "I cannot believe my own ears."

"And how about those times when you didn't have to go to the emergency room?"

"Such as?" I noticed that however fast I walked he kept a step or two ahead of me. He was pretty good with his cane. I did not believe that he was seriously awkward.

"Such as when you walked into the tree branch and cut yourself above the eye. I can still see the scar. Last summer. And the time you spilled hot coffee on your lap? Also last summer. Are you just awkward, or are you trying to tell me something? I need to know, David. This is my life as well as yours."

"You want me to see a shrink. You think I have a major personality disorder. My God, Dannie, I'm only human. Maybe a human klutz but still a human."

"Listen to us," I said. "We're not even married and we're having one of those on-the-brink conversations. I can't bear it. No, I don't really think you need a shrink; I don't know why I said that. David, you're walking too fast — I can't keep up with you."

"Sorry," he said. "Look, I think we both need to cool down." He reached into his pocket for the key to the front door. He turned the key, opened the door and stood back to allow me to go in first.

"Thanks for the nice dinner," I said.

Later, in bed, neither of us could sleep and neither of us spoke. The room was dark except for the stripe of wan light thrown up by the streetlamp. David's hand found its way to my left breast. He knew what to do there. "I've got a confession to make," he said so softly I made him repeat what he had said.

I told him that he didn't have to tell me anything. But he insisted. "You were mostly right about this accident thing. I never told you why Betty and I split up, did I?"

"You said something about going in different directions."

He said that was putting it mildly. The real story emerged with many hesitations, throat clearings, and sighs. He and his wife Betty and their two children were driving to Baltimore to visit Betty's sister's family over Thanksgiving. David and the sister were not the best of friends. He thought she had an attitude problem — "bossy, she couldn't help telling everyone what to do" — but this was a trip Betty very much wanted to make. The children were quite young: Josh was nine and Rachel seven. It was getting late and they had to decide whether to stop at a motel or drive through until they got there. David wanted to stop for the night; Betty persuaded him to go on. It was only another hour to go. The children, she pointed out, were already asleep in the back seat. Why wake them now? David yielded. About six miles from their destination, having left the highway, David drove through a suburban intersection. A pickup truck, coming from the right, hit their car broadside, plowing into the right rear door, which crunched and buckled, injuring Rachel. "I apologize for not going into any more details," he said. I told him I didn't need them. "You see," he said, "there was a stop sign but it was obscured by some trees. But I should have stopped or at least slowed down before the intersection. It was my fault. We thought Rachel was going to die. She had a concussion and her leg and hip were broken. She was in a cast for months. She's okay now, she's learned how to compensate. You'd like her." David paused. "Incidentally, she doesn't blame me."

"And her mother?" I said, seeing all too vividly the scene as David described it.

"That's another story," he said. "Rachel survived. The marriage didn't."

What had I got myself into? I'd fallen for a man who couldn't — or wouldn't — keep himself safe. Tempting fate and wanting someone close to stanch the bleeding. In kind, he was no different from Evel Knievel, or the Frenchman who walked across a tightrope connecting the two World Trade towers. Not in kind, only in degree. David was telling me this without coming right out and saying so. And so what? An inner voice started peppering me with questions: "Is this sufficient to split? Does David do drugs? Does he fuck other women? Does he cuff you around? Does he drink himself into a stupor? Does he blow his paycheck at the track? Then what are you bitching about? He may be a little goofy, a little needy, but he's one of the good guys. He's a sweetheart. This accident thing — it has nothing to do with you. You can live with it."

I realized that David had gone to sleep without bestowing his usual kiss.

The next morning at breakfast, David was subdued. "Should I not have told you?" he asked. "I'm sorry I told you."

"Of course you should have told me. You should have told me long ago. But we won't talk about it anymore if it makes you unhappy," I said.

"I don't deserve you," David said.

"Please don't misread me," I told him. "It isn't helpful."

David said he understood perfectly when I told him, later that day, that I needed some time by myself. Besides, I had just about decided to accept Raymie's offer. It was odd and wondrous, how the more jobs

I took on — it was now three: the house book with Beth, the *Peter Pan* project and Raymie and Mitch's trophy house — the more energy I seemed to have. I had, meanwhile, told various book editors that I was taking a "vacation" from other illustration work until my own book was finished.

Beth came to join me in Truro, bringing Marshall, who kissed me on the lips and wagged his tail for five minutes before he knocked a glass of juice off the coffee table. Beth was in very good spirits. She had had her hair expensively cut and shaped. She was wearing real clothes, not sweats. She told me she had been going online to meet guys. I stifled any show of doubt about this. After all, I knew several women who had met their mates on the Internet. Still, it seemed a risky way of doing that sort of business. "How do you know they're not going to lure you somewhere secluded and dark and rape you?"

"Mom! This is two thousand and three. This is the way it's done. Sure there are creeps on the Internet. But there are plenty of creeps in real life too."

At least she wasn't still living with that married person. I think she kicked him out.

Beth had brought her text with her and we matched it up with my pictures. This took over two hours. "I really like this," I said. "I think we've done a good job. I hope David likes it."

Beth asked if I was going to marry David. "I don't know, pet, I can't make up my mind. He wants to. I try to like New York but it's so noisy. I can't get used to the noise. I miss the quiet. And I miss Marshall. I hope he isn't any trouble?" I thought, "How can a dog not be trouble?" But Beth shook her head. And then she asked me if it was just the noise or something else I couldn't get used to. I told her she sounded like a shrink. The phone rang. It was Raymie asking me when I was going to come over. "You said you'd be here at eleven. It's almost twelve." I told her Beth was with me. "Bring her."

Beth didn't want to come with me. She said she didn't like anything about this trophy house project. "You've lost it, Mom."

"No, Beth, I haven't. It's a compromise. I don't want to lose Raymie. If I say no, she won't understand." A blush of incredulity spread over Beth's face. How could I persuade her that, at my age, principles could easily be trumped by friendship? I think maybe it's something you learn only by living through those moments when you have to choose one or the other. Most of the time, it didn't matter. But what if your closest friend asked you to hide her secret that she had sold military secrets to the North Koreans? Or that she was guilty of a hit-and-run accident, killing an old lady? Or that she had gone to Neiman Marcus, where she had acquired a number of small items, none of which she had paid for? I suppose one answer would be that this is not a friend you would want to see any more of. This is a sociopath and you can't trust them. But in my case, now, to put it into the category of moral dilemma was dignifying it beyond its worth. As far as I could tell, it was no big deal. And maybe converting the Brenner house into a B&B would take some of the curse off it. Beth said, "I don't see how you can take part in Raymie's horrible scheme. You hate that house, you hate what it stands for, you hate the greed that oozes out of every crack."

"But I love Raymie. I'm afraid I need her in my old age."

"Mom, you're not old! You're not even sixty."

"Thanks."

"No, really, Mom, this isn't like you. It's got something to do with Dad, doesn't it?"

I told her I couldn't really tell what had caused the slippage from a moral stance to something a good deal more pragmatic. I also said that my so-called moral issues were as nothing compared to what was going on in the Middle East — wars on all sides; wholesale slaughter.

"You don't give a shit, do you?"

"Well, actually I do give a shit," I told her. "But it's not large enough to make Raymie hate me. Besides, it might be a hoot. I can buy whatever I want — money being no object — take as many pictures with film bought by someone else, furnish rooms I'd never live in myself but which I think I can make presentable if not actually beautiful. Who am I hurting?"

With the certitude of the young, Beth said that I was hurting myself. And I told her that maybe, when she got to be my age, she'd find out what I was talking about. She seethed. She was angrier than I'd seen her in a long time. "And now, I'm going over there to ink the pact," I said. "You can come or not, as you please." I was pretty ticked off myself, which just goes to show how hard it had been for me to make up my mind — and how ambivalent I still felt. I put on a good show for my daughter, but I hadn't entirely convinced myself. But that was okay too. I was looking forward to spending someone else's money.

CHAPTER 11

Walking over unyielding sand toward the Brenner house, I realized — abruptly and with a touch of denial — that whenever things got rough, I retreated alone to Cape Cod. It bothered me that I had done the same thing over and over again without having been fully aware of it. This only reinforced the doleful fact that most of the time we don't know squat about why we do the things we do. The rest of the time we're at the mercy of creatures crawling around in the murk below, far below. Not that there was anything wrong with my retreat; it was less expensive than shopping, less destructive than drinking. All the same, I would have liked to be consciously brave and up to the challenge of trying to figure out what I wanted.

The opposite of a beach resort, Truro in late March requires a kind of tempered stoicism. Not too many people have the stomach for it. I didn't see myself as a bleak sort of person, but as cheerful with just a pinch of sadness. The more I covered myself with solitude, the better I felt. Simply put, I liked being alone. I can't really count Marshall, although he's the best company there is.

The tide was going out. Crescents of sea grass lay on the shore in a perfect rhythm that echoed the waves. The sky was studded with clouds and the sun was unusually bright for this time of year. My cheeks began to burn.

It took me about just under ten minutes of vigorous walking to get to what I had already begun to think of as Trophy House — not as a trophy house but as an institution. Marshall took one look at Mitch's poodle, Rambo, and tried to get back outside. I told him it was okay, I'd see that Rambo didn't hurt him. Raymie poured champagne into a flute and handed it to me. I don't really like champagne; it makes my head hurt. But it's the drink to solemnize significant occasions with so I accepted and sipped. Mitch came limping into the room. "Well, well," he said, "here's our newest washashore." There was something ironic about this man patronizing me in these terms; he had barely established himself as a Truroite and here he was, greeting me like a newcomer, I who had lived here for thirty years, on and off. But it was this "on and off" that had kept me from being a washashore. To be a true washashore you had to live here year-round, perpetually, through the bleak winter, through periods where no sun ever shines, where the wind gets down your throat, when even the dog won't go out-side. During the "season" it means living with the day-trippers and renters who get into fistfights in the parking lot at Ballston Beach and who buy all their groceries at Jellies, the Cartier of convenience stores.

"You know, Mitch, I still haven't decided to live here year-round. I have this friend in New York —"

"Her boyfriend," Raymie said, inter-rupting me. "He wants them to get mar-ried."

"Why get married?" Mitch said. "Look at Raymie and me. We get along great. Why fix something that ain't broken?"

"You mean why buy a cow when milk is so cheap, don't you?" Raymie said. Mitch went over to Raymie and fingered her bottom. At least I think that's what he did; you couldn't be sure, it happened so fast. But Raymie smiled indulgently.

"Drink up," Mitch said to me. "That's the real French McCoy."

"Mitch, Dannie doesn't have to be told."

Mitch invited me to sit down. I picked one of the leather armchairs. He asked me whether I'd decided to help them design the best little B&B on the East Coast — maybe in the whole US of A?

Raymie said, "That's why she's here, Mitch."

"Well then, let's get down to business."

"Can I ask you something, Mitch?" He looked at me with a trace of impatience. "Why do you want me to do this when there are plenty of professional decorators looking for work?"

Was I fishing? No doubt. He told me that he and Raymie had chosen me because, as he put it, "you're an artiste, you have an eye for what goes well with what, you're not just out to rob the client blind." At this, he pulled out a contract for me to read over and then sign. Every possible — and some implausible — contingencies had been included. I asked him if a lawyer had worked it up. "You betcha," he said. "I don't expect my lawyer to manage hotels. I don't know much about drawing up a contract. I believe in getting the best advice. Experts." I nodded. It was all right with me if my being "deceased" was one of the contingencies. Raymie said, "Mitch leaves nothing to chance, do you, honey?"

I immediately thought of Lyle Halliday. "Did they ever catch Halliday?" I said.

Mitch said, "How did you know? They apprehended him day before yesterday. He was living in this run-down cabin or shack house with about a dozen other whacked-out, like-minded individuals." These were, he said, mostly men along with a few women (I figured them to be the food gatherers and dishwashers) who wanted to keep the earth pristine but also to wipe "mongrel" races off its face.

"It's about time we were mongrelized," I said.

"Whatever," Mitch said. I don't think he found this such a cool idea. "The little prick hates Jews, African-Americans, Asians, Hispanics."

"Latinos, Mitch," Raymie said. "They want to be called 'Latinos.'"

"Whatever," Mitch said. "In any case, these folks had a lot of firearms and manuals on how to manufacture explosives. They also found stacks of flyers — you know, the kind someone put on car windshields parked at Corn Hill last summer."

I said it was weird, the combination of environmentalist and neo-Nazi in the same person. Mitch said, "When you think about it, it isn't that weird. They don't want anyone doing stuff to the land."

"They want to keep it for Aryans?" I said.

"And get this," Raymie said. "This guy had a prior record. When he was a little kid, he'd been put away for a while for zapping small animals in his mother's microwave oven."

"That's cute," I said, unable to block the picture my imagination produced. It was a black kitten. I felt sick.

"They're out there," Mitch said, as if that made it all right. "What say we talk about our expectations for this house? We're counting on you to make it a show-place." I told him I would try not to disappoint him, although "showplace" was not exactly what I had in mind. I was still so rattled by the image of the kitten exploding inside the microwave that I had a hard time focusing.

Raymie took over: "We want this place to be elegant but not showy," she said.

"I don't know what you mean by 'showy,'" Mitch said.

"Of course you do, honey. Just think Ruthie." This must have penetrated because Mitch nodded.

"I guess Raymie told you, we want to pay you handsomely for a handsome job.

This fee doesn't include whatever monies you spend on furniture and the like. We also want you to keep an accurate record of everything you spend and on what. I mean, not just 'bed,' but a description of the particular bed." Was he being nitpicky? No doubt, but it was his money so I guess he was entitled.

We went over the contract sentence by sentence. My stomach growled just as Raymie said, "I'm going to fix us some lunch."

As soon as she left the room, Mitch asked me if I didn't think Raymie was the best little old gal anyone could want to spend their days with. "She's a regular jewel." I smiled. Whether she was the best little gal or not, it was very nice that he thought so; it would make things easier as time lurched on.

The lunch Raymie fixed was delicious and obviously planned well ahead: squash soup, crab cakes, mesclun salad, berries (frozen, thawed). Mitch and Raymie ate well. We talked for a while about my ideas for the house. I hoped to persuade them that I had given a good deal of thought to the matter but was in fact improvising as the soup went down. "I see mostly white, blue, and a bit of pale yellow." I went on to say that the markup of antiques anywhere on the Cape was out of sight. On the other hand, if you bought things off-Cape, you paid an exorbitant price to get them trucked over the bridge.

"Six of one, half a dozen of the other, eh?" Mitch said. "Look, Dannie," he said, in a different tone altogether. "I don't want to micromanage this project. That's why we hired you."

I caught Raymie's eye. She nodded almost imperceptibly. "Right," I said. "I understand."

When I got back to the house, Beth was on the phone. She hung up when she saw me. Marshall went over and nudged her crotch. "Go away," she said. "Nasty dog."

"Who were you talking to?"

"Dad," she said.

"That's nice, I'm glad you're in touch." I was dying to know what they had talked about but I didn't ask; I held my tongue, difficult though it was.

Beth wanted to know how it went. "I still can't believe you're doing this."

I told her it went swimmingly. I told her what we had talked about and stopped short of saying that I thought that Mitch, for all his gnomelike sensibilities, was not as awful as I once believed him to be. Could I have lived with him? No. Could I work with him? Probably. He struck me as being basically sensible when it came to business.

"Don't you want to know why I called Dad?"

"Sure. Okay."

"I called to wish him happy birthday," she said.

"Oh my God. March twenty-first!"

"It's okay, Mom. You're divorced. You don't have to remember."

"I remembered for thirty-five years," I said. Beth came over and threw her arms around me. I began to cry. She stayed with me until I calmed down, then she went off to Provincetown, to do what, I had no idea.

I could no longer put off making up my mind. I had brought my *Peter Pan* work with me and worked like a beaver, chewing her way through log after log. It was going reasonably well. David called me twice a day, once before I started working, and again late in the afternoon as the sun sped toward darkness. The shoreline of the bay on the Outer Cape is the only place on the East Coast where the sun seems to set into the water. People come from all over, park their cars as close as they can get to the actual beach, and watch this display with open mouth. It's easy to see why: wonder and resolution at the same moment.

Around six o'clock, while Beth and I watched the news, David phoned. He told me he wanted me to come back to New York. "What else is new?" I said.

"That's mean," he said. "Why are you doing this?"

"I'm sorry," I said. "I thought you'd take it as a joke. I meant it as a joke."

"I don't know," he said.

"What don't you know?" I didn't wait for his answer but told him I was planning to come back to New York in a couple of days, when "we have to talk."

"That sounds ominous," David said.

"It doesn't have to be," I said, knowing it was. What lay ahead reminded me of a line from a 1930s Fred Astaire–Ginger Rogers movie, spoken earnestly by a Slavic malaprop: "It's time to face the musicians."

"The musicians" was this choice: either I marry David or cut myself loose. It cannot be true, as I have been told, that if you have genuine trouble trying to decide between A and B, then it doesn't matter which one you choose. For a while I had been almost, but not quite, persuaded by this bit of sophistry. I loved David but I was almost fifty-four. I didn't see me fitting into the mold of newlywed. It was too goopy. It was too complicated. Tom could easily take all that on. In hindsight, I viewed my ex-husband (I think objectively) as oblivious to most of the complications life tosses at you without discrimination or fairness. He just went on doing his thing — and making it work out for him. It wasn't like that for me. David was wonderful; every time I saw him afresh I melted exactly the way Beth had when Andy pleaded with her to come back to him. That lure is more dangerous than a riptide, especially when sex is in the mix, mainly because you can't get your head straight.

As I looked out the train window, I saw ugly Bridgeport through a film of tears. How do you know, until after your big chance has come and gone, what makes you happy — or some reasonable facsimile? By then it's too late. "I never knew what true happiness was until I was married — and then it was too late." This is a joke my father used to tell my mother from time to time until she ordered him not to repeat it again. "It's stopped being funny, Ted," she told him.

The minute I walked into David's apartment, I knew I just couldn't live there. The place didn't smell like home, and an air strange and unfriendly surrounded me, as if I were seeing it for the first time. There was his couch, his lamp, his art on the walls — he liked abstractions with broad patches of muted color that bled into each other. They were perfectly okay of their kind, but they weren't what I would have bought — too hidden. David was waiting for me. He was wearing a sweatshirt and chinos and hadn't shaved for a couple of days — a Tom Cruise sort of look that turns me on. "Come here and give us a kiss," he said as soon as I put my bag down. As soon as our mouths convened, he started trying to pull off my jacket. "David," I said.

"What is it?"

I told him I thought we should wait until later. He wanted to know when later was. "Just later," I said.

"I thought something like this was going to happen," he said. He was having trouble talking.

"You did?"

"Of course. Do you think I can't read signals? Do you think I'm stupid?"

I suppose there was something healthy in

his mounting anger; it was a better reaction than crying would have been.

"David, let's go out somewhere nice and try to plan something. I can't live in New York, you know that, and you can't just quit everything and live in Truro. You don't like it that much anyway. We'll figure something out."

He said he really appreciated my positive attitude. Before my eyes, the ugly side of David came crawling out from where it had been. In a sense, it was a relief, as I had thought him — aside from the accident thing — almost any woman's ideal man. So he was not above playing dirty when I had hurt him. We traded sarcasm, each giving as good as he or she got, then stopped suddenly as I decided that I didn't want to leave him with this foul taste in my mouth. "Please, David, let's not do this anymore. Please let's try to . . ." I stopped, unable to say "end on a lovely note." He made a snorting noise at this. "You must be nuts," he said. "Would you say you have been stringing me along all this time?"

"I would say I haven't," I said. "Maybe I'm not like other women. I need more than a man to go to bed with and to eat breakfast with." David said I sounded like a feminist of the 1970s. "My postfeminist friends would never say such a silly thing."

"Silly? Okay, if that's what you want to think." And all the time my body was cramping with sexual desire. I could hardly stand it. What was I doing? "But Dannie," I told myself, "the sex act occupies, at best, only a few hours a week. What about the rest of the time? Are you going to live in this city and forsake your home for a few hours of exquisite pleasure? You are? I don't believe you. Anyway, if you married David, the sex would stop being so cool after a while. Then where will you be?"

David headed into the bedroom — our bedroom! — saying, over his shoulder, that he was going to change his pants and put on a pair of shoes. He and I were going out for a "last supper."

We went to an upscale fish restaurant — no one was wearing a lobster bib — and it was, miraculously, quiet, in spite of the fact that almost every table was occupied. We each ordered a drink and sat mooning at each other. "It's not the end of the world," I said.

"Whose world is it not the end of?"

"Neither mine nor yours," I said. "Now let's just try to be with each other without saying anything hurtful. I'm as sad about this as you are — maybe more so."

"I doubt that."

I asked him if we could possibly work out a compromise, an idea that had been at the edge of my consciousness for a while and which the martini I had ordered shoved into clarity. I articulated the idea. He loved New York City. I loved Cape Cod. We loved each other, we loved each other's company, so why couldn't we continue to be together as often as we possibly could, given the expense and the distance between the two places. We would trade weekends. He could spend his vacation with me in Truro, I would take the train or bus or hitch a ride to New York whenever I felt I could take a breather in my work. "I don't want to stop seeing you."

"But I want to be with you all the time."

"It's not possible," I said. "This will be the best of two worlds. We won't get bored with each other this way. Maybe, in another twenty years or so, we'll both end up in the same place. I'll pick up things for you when you can't bend over anymore. You'll read the *New York Times* to me when I can't see anymore."

"What if I meet someone else?" he said. He had barely touched his sole.

"That's a chance I'll have to take," I said.

CHAPTER 12

David adjusted to our new arrangement with a speed that, while it failed to squeeze tears of anguish from my eyes, didn't, on the other hand, suggest that I had reason to celebrate. What could his recovery mean but that he wasn't heartbroken enough to fall into a depression, or come after me with a pistol and threaten to shoot me — "If I can't have you, then I'll see to it that no one can" — or even that he couldn't work or sleep. Basically, I'd rejected him, but he seemed to rally the way he might have if he'd eaten a plate of rotten fish; it only takes three days or so to get the bad stuff out of your system. When I proposed it, I wasn't sure at all that he would agree to return to a long-distance romance. But his e-mails and cheery phone calls suggested he had made a near-miraculous recovery from being dumped. In fact, we both thrived. Every time we were together, whether in New York or Truro, I was stung by the same craving for his affection — in all its forms, all the way from raw sex to explicit approval, something I realized Tom had been stingy with — yet, how could I have known this without something to compare it to? The arrangement turned out to be a model solution. Beth claimed not to understand, but that's because she was, I guess, more conventional than I am; she would have liked there to be a clean resolution: either split or marry. This was messier, more ambiguous, but in its own way more satisfying, mainly because it combined intense desire with intense pleasure. It was never, not for a minute, boring.

I can hardly remember what we did before e-mail slid into our lives. For one thing, it's a shortcut; you don't have to crack the shell in order to get to the meat. It has the virtue of instancy, even more than the telephone, which depends on both of you being in the same mood at the same time. It lets you be raw, unlike a letter, where you have to craft sentences and make sure they parse. David and I e-mailed each other several times a day. Some of his messages were love letters, some hilarious descriptions of problems at the publishing house, some had to do with food, others with his children. Some of them were just right for the *Times*' Metropolitan Diary. He seemed to have no hang-ups when engaging in this form of communication. And I guess I was equally forthcoming. I let him know — for the first time — how I really felt about his accidents. It wasn't, I explained, that he *had* them but that I didn't have the stamina to take care of him when they occurred. I wanted both of us to be equally resilient — at least at this point in my life. When I get older — if I get older — I wouldn't mind looking after him. But not yet. I hoped he'd wait.

One of his (ungrammatical) e-mails said: "While this fucking Bush war is going full steam — and having screwed the U.N. — your New York admirer is turning inward and seeing a shrink once a week. Don't laugh. Don't say I told you so. It's not as painful as I thought it would be. She doesn't want to know about my mother or my potty training (I remember it vividly!) as much as my day-to-day hang-ups. She wants to know about you. I wish she'd do more of the talking. More later."

I wondered if she were pretty, like Dr. Melfi on *The Sopranos.* Dr. Melfi had great legs, which she crossed in a manner that could only arouse poor Tony's lust. I wondered if David's shrink had great legs. I asked him about the legs in my next e-mail and he answered back that he had no idea.

That had to be a lie.

Meanwhile, I was tutoring myself in the buying of antiques. I went to a couple of shows, one in Boston, one in Rhinebeck, New York, spread out over the Dutchess County Fairgrounds. Some of the stuff was spectacular. I wanted to know why it had ended up in a tent rather than in the houses of the owners' children. Hard times? A rejection of their parents' style and taste? I bought some books and magazines. I talked to people who seemed to know about how you decide what's substantial and what's going to fall apart. I liked seven-foot-high bureaus and hefty beds. I liked washstands with a hole for the basin. I hated stripes on anything. I was tempted to ask Raymie to help me decide whether or not to buy a sleigh bed from a dealer in Chatham, on the Cape. It was twenty-five hundred dollars. Even if the money wasn't coming out of my bank balance, I balked at paying so much for a bed. I finally told the owner of Chatham Antiquities — who told me right off the bat to call him Guy — that I would like to buy the bed. He said, "You're making a very wise choice; this is one of the finest examples of nineteenth-century craftsmanship I've seen in ages. I believe William Howard Taft slept in it — all three hundred pounds of him."

"You told me that the last time I was here," I said, smiling so that his feelings wouldn't be hurt. I wondered why he felt he had to keep selling the bed after I agreed to buy it. Guy stroked the headboard. "Feel the luster," he said, examining his palm. "Where is this handsome piece going?" he asked, almost as if he were reluctant to lose it.

"Truro," I said.

"Oh my," he said. "That *is* a ways." Not really, I told him. A matter of less than an hour. He said he had a mover who worked for him two days a week. Any day would be fine, I said, since this is going into a bed-and-breakfast that isn't going to be open for business for a while yet. "A B&B," he said. "Oh dear. I hope you're not going to allow smoking in your establishment."

"It's not mine," I said. "I'm just the person buying the furniture." I refused to identify myself as an interior decorator. "Why didn't you tell me you were a decorator?" Guy said. "I would have taken a little something off the price." I told him I wasn't a professional but was doing this for friends. If I had been told a year and a half earlier that I would ever refer to Mitch Brenner as a friend, I would have sneered,

"In a pig's eye." And now look.

Mitch and Raymie were crazy about the bed. "Sturdy enough for a fat president," I said. "I have my eye on a canopy bed in Yarmouthport."

There was a lot to do. I was finishing *Peter Pan*; the editor was pleased with my work but kept tweaking things. He objected to the nose I gave Peter — too adult. He objected to the dimples I gave Wendy. "Too cute. Dimples are out." He asked me to deepen the colors — too pastel for what he had in mind. He was the most demanding editor I had ever worked with and it made me doubt my own competence. If he didn't like my stuff, why did he choose me? A couple of times I considered dropping the project and giving the money back. David told me not to. "I know this person," he said. "He's one of the best. His books — every other year at least one prize. Stick with it." I wanted to hug him but I was sitting at my laptop.

I bought furnishings for the house with deliberate slowness. Mitch kept at me. "At this rate, the place won't be open until next summer. Can't have that."

"You weren't seriously thinking of having guests this summer?"

"I was."

I told him, sure, if he wanted me to buy the first thing I saw, okay, but it wouldn't be what he wanted. "I've got to take my time," I said. Raymie and I took a long walk on the beach during which I asked her to help put the brakes on Mitch. She promised. I felt a rush of warmth for my friend, who had, incidentally, dropped the preppy look and was more than halfway back to her old style of old clothes: aged jeans and a ratty old sweater. I wondered if Mitch had noticed the slippage.

The brochure was a rush job, but it came out fairly well, with my photograph (I wanted black and white, Mitch wanted color; I did color) of Trophy House on the front cover and, inside, a view of the beach and another of the deck with tables and chairs arranged prettily, potted flowers on the tables, cushions on the chairs and a boiled lobster at each place setting. I told him I felt funny about the lobster pictures — we were a B&B, after all; dinner was not included. "No one'll make that connection," Mitch said. "The lobsters give the place extra class — not that it needs it." None of my pictures had the slightest suggestion of ambiguity or bad weather. Mitch loved my work. Trophy House was a paradise within a paradise. He had several thousand brochures printed in Boston and distributed them to travel agents and chambers of commerce. And halfway through August, when I had finally finished buying beds, bedside tables, chairs, love seats, bureaus, towels, sheets, curtains, rugs, vases and pitchers, bowls and potpourri, he hired a Webmaster who designed a Trophy House Web site. We were off and running. I had become a constituent of the enterprise.

Mitch decided to celebrate the grand opening of Trophy House with a Labor Day bash. "I know we don't have much time," he said, "but I'm going to open with as many dogs and ponies as I can round up." Raymie said, "Mitch, Labor Day's only two weeks away. We can't possibly do this in two weeks."

"I thought you knew me, baby," he said, squinting his eyes into a love twinkle. "Just you watch."

Mitch engaged a Boston publicity person at an inflated price. Raymie reported that the woman — her outfit was Synergy by Sylvia — doubled her fee because this job meant she would have to stop working for her other clients for two weeks. "Mitch was okay with that," Raymie said. "I told him that people in Truro hated publicity. You know what he said? He said, 'They'll like this.' " Mitch obtained a list of every registered voter in Wellfleet, Truro, and North Truro and instructed Sylvia to send out invitations to every one of them by e-mail. Sylvia argued that printed invitations were more appropriate. Mitch said getting them made would take too long. She was skeptical but, as she told Raymie, "It's his money, it's his party." The invitation asked them to "help inaugurate Trophy House, the only world-class Bed-and-Breakfast on the East Coast, featuring a spectacular view of Cape Cod Bay and equally spectacular sunsets. Once your friends stay here, they will never want to spend a week anywhere else." With this last blandishment he had hooked into the Truroite's dread of houseguests. Houseguests had a way of spending more time in your house than they were invited for. He hired my son Mark's rock group, Dandruff, to play for three hours. The food was to be catered by Puff Pastry, a place in Provincetown that specialized in gay and lesbian parties, figuring, as he said, "that those folks really care about good food, and know how to present it." He rented four all-terrain vehicles and four young hunks to drive them from the two closest public lots, where guests could park, up (or down) the beach to the foot of Mitch's stairs.

I found myself caught up in the excitement; then I stepped back and wondered what the hell I was a part of. Distressed by the Brenner style, so antithetical to what washashores and wannabes cherished, I still viewed Mitch as a panther who had crept into the aviary. I called David and told him about my misgivings. He asked if he was invited to the party. "Of course you are," I said. "What do you think?"

"I'm looking forward to it," David said. "You're taking this too seriously."

"You don't understand."

"I think I do," he said.

Where do you go from this? I told him Beth was disgusted with me. "She thinks I've sold out to the enemy. As far as I'm concerned, the enemy [I was thinking of the way this country had turned from a nice, somewhat naïve kid into a cynical bully] is far worse than Mitch Brenner. At least he wants to do something about his mistake." David said that Beth would probably get over her attack of ideals. "I'll bet she comes to the party."

"I'll bet she doesn't. What are we wagering?"

"There's nothing I really want," he said. "Except you." I figured he meant it maybe about sixty percent.

Mitch was delighted when most of Truro's washashores showed up at his party. Not only year-rounders who lived here in well-insulated houses back in the woods and away from the most howling of winds, but some folks who actually worked here: off-duty policemen, employees of the library and Town Hall, owners of big dark restaurants on or just off Route 6, and a couple of motel owners. Every segment of this insular winter community was represented. I caught a glimpse of Norman Mailer and his wife and a couple of small children, one of whom he introduced as "Wiggy." Still, I was certain that what drew these people to the party was more curiosity than a desire to help Mitchell Brenner celebrate. Truro folks wanted to check out the house and declare it showy, impossible. Raymie drank wine nervously. Mitch was wearing white loafers with no socks, a blue cotton blazer and a captain's hat with a visor. Mark and his group played loudly, numbers that sounded great but that I couldn't have named if you held my toes to the fire. David talked to Raymie and my *Peter Pan* editor. The food — a raw bar of cherrystones and oysters, small triangular spinach pies, chicken wings, cheese and onion roll-ups, slices of smoked salmon on black bread — couldn't have been better. The waiters and clam shuckers wore pink cotton jackets and white pants. Mitch invited his guests, only a few of whom he actually knew by name, to inspect the place. People formed an orderly line and made their way through the house, subdued, as if they were in a national shrine or a famous writer's abode. I placed myself in back of a woman I didn't know who, with her husband, I had heard making a remark about Mitch's having greased a couple of palms to get a business variance. But when she saw the first of my rooms, she said: "This is perfectly lovely. I would stay in this room myself. Who would have thought it, from the outside?" I slipped away.

With a glass of champagne in his hand, Mitch Brenner welcomed his guests; several of them stared at their shoes while he talked. Their loss. They will never be willing to give a man like Mitchell Brenner an even break, so why try to win them over? They have nasty, chilly little souls. I wanted to go step on their feet. David came up behind me and nudged my shoulder with his cheek. "Look who's coming up the beach," he said.

It was Beth. She was striding up the beach with — oh my God — Pete Savage, the P'Town cop. Something terrible must have happened. Had Halliday struck again? I ran to the top of the stairs and as soon as she got into hearing distance I called out to her, "Beth, are you okay?"

She looked a little sheepish. "Pete and I wanted to see what kind of circus Brenner puts on," she said. She let me give her a hug. "I left my things at the house, Mom. I can stay 'til early tomorrow morning." She grinned at Pete.

"Do you mind if I ask you something? I didn't know you two even knew each other . . ." I paused, scrambling for words. "Are you two an item?"

"An item? Mom, this is century twenty-one. But yes, as a matter of fact, we're seeing each other." And as she said this, their eyes locked. Pete Savage, a short, compact person with a shaved head, an earring, and a decent smile, looked as if he enjoyed sex, food, and apprehending male-factors to the fullest. Whether or not he sprang from blue-collar stock didn't espe-cially interest me, though, to be perfectly honest, he had the earmarks. His beefy hands, for one thing, and a certain nondefined quality to his chin and nose. I'm not a snob, I'm merely describing. At this point in my daughter's life, all I wanted was for her to find a guy who (a) wouldn't beat her up, (b) wouldn't ignore her, (c) didn't drink to excess, and, should she choose to have a child, (d) would be a loving father. If his own father had caught and filleted fish for a living, that was fine with me.

I hadn't asked them how they met, but Beth was good at reading my mind. "We met at a party in P'Town," she said. "He was standing on the deck all by himself with this disgusting purple drink in his hand. He didn't look like he was having a very good time. So I just went up to him and started talking and — the rest is history." She gave him a look of unmistakable love. He put his arm around her still-slim waist and drew her against his hip. "Your daughter is a wonderful person, Mrs. Faber," he said. "But you already know that."

Beth seemed embarrassed by Pete's directness. "Is David here?"

I nodded. "He's around here somewhere. Would you like to see the inside of the house?"

I took Beth and Pete on a tour of the guest rooms, while trying to regain my balance, which Beth had knocked me off. She was mostly silent, but I could tell she liked the rooms. I was prepared for her to say something like "What a waste," but she didn't. "You did okay," she said finally. Back outside, Beth dropped another bombshell: "I'm going to open a wedding planner business in P'Town." She must have seen my surprise. "It's okay, Mom," she said (while all the time basking in the light of her newfound lover's love). "I've done a lot of research and I know exactly what it entails. I applied to the Cape Cod Five for a small business loan." Here, Pete interrupted: "They liked the cut of Beth's jib," he said admiringly. "They approved the loan." She said that a lot of people thought that same-sex marriage was going to be legalized within a year. "Gays and lesbians — don't ask me why, I really don't understand it — want to do it the most traditional way. They want all the trappings — gold rings, a three-tiered cake, formal clothes, matchbooks with their names intertwined, a catered, sit-down dinner. The works."

"Sounds to me like they want to outstraight us straights," I said. "Are you sure it's not a put-on?"

"Yes, I'm sure. They're very serious. A lot of them have done it already — only without it being legal. But that's going to change. I'm getting in on the ground floor, so to speak. There's a shitload of money in weddings."

"What do you think of all this?" I asked Pete.

"I think it's a great idea," he said. I had the impression that he would find any idea of Beth's a great idea.

"Does one of the two change his or her name?" I said.

"What do you mean?" Beth said.

"Like in a straight marriage. The woman usually takes her husband's name."

"Whatever," Beth said, abruptly switching gears. "I want a bunch of those clams. C'mon, Pete, let's eat!"

David said he knew Beth would show up. "She really loves you."

"Sometimes I'm not so sure," I said, starting to tear up. I told him about Beth's two pieces of news.

"Good for her," he said.

"It probably won't last," I said. "What are she and the cop going to talk about?"

"Crime and prime ribs. I hope in equal amounts," David said.

"I should let go?"

David nodded. "What is it you really want?" he asked.

"If only I knew." And then it came to me: "I suppose this." I nodded toward the west. "I think this is the most beautiful place in the whole world. Of course I haven't seen the whole world but enough of it to know this ranks right up there. My legs go soft when I look out over the bay and watch the water moving softly like a dream. You're going to think I'm nuts, but sometimes it's almost pornographic. Do you know what I mean?"

David nodded. "I don't think you're nuts. Just, is it enough?"

"I used to think it should make me happier, more excited, more hopeful. And, bad as it was — and still is — I don't think this mood is really connected to September eleventh. I guess I'm like one of those Henry James characters, where happiness is just around the next corner. You're not like that, David."

"I'm not?" he said. "Are you absolutely sure you don't want to be your daughter's first client?"

ABOUT THE AUTHOR

ANNE BERNAYS is a novelist (including *Professor Romeo* and *Growing Up Rich*), and co-author, with her husband, Justin Kaplan, of *Back Then: Two Lives in 1950s New York.* Her articles, book reviews and essays have appeared in such major publications as the *New York Times*, *Sports Illustrated*, and the *Nation.* A longtime teacher of writing, she is co-author, with Pamela Painter, of the textbook *What If?* Ms. Bernays currently teaches at Harvard's Nieman Foundation. She and Mr. Kaplan have six grandchildren. They live in Cambridge, Massachusetts, and Truro, Cape Cod.

The employees of Thorndike Press hope you have enjoyed this Large Print book. All our Thorndike and Wheeler Large Print titles are designed for easy reading, and all our books are made to last. Other Thorndike Press Large Print books are available at your library, through selected bookstores, or directly from us.

For information about titles, please call:

(800) 223-1244

or visit our Web site at:

www.gale.com/thorndike
www.gale.com/wheeler

To share your comments, please write:

Publisher
Thorndike Press
295 Kennedy Memorial Drive
Waterville, ME   04901

16